Spotting
the
Leopard

ANNA MYERS

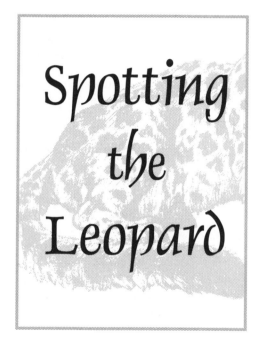

Spotting
the
Leopard

WALKER AND COMPANY

New York

First published in the United States of America in 1996 by Walker Publishing Company, Inc.

Published simultaneously in Canada by Thomas Allen & Son Canada, Limited, Markham, Ontario

Library of Congress Cataloging-in-Publication Data
Myers, Anna.
Spotting the leopard/Anna Myers.
p.   cm.
Sequel to: Red-dirt Jessie.
Summary: In the late 1930s, H. J. Harper is intent on finding a way to help his older sister study to become a veterinarian and on tracking down a leopard that has escaped from the zoo in Oklahoma City where his father is working on a W.P.A. project.
ISBN 0-8027-8459-3
[1. Family life—Oklahoma—Fiction.
2. Brothers and sisters—Fiction.
3. Leopards—Fiction. 4. Oklahoma—Fiction.]
I. Title.
PZ7.M9814Sp   1996
[Fic]—dc20   96-13697
                                 CIP
                                 AC

Book design by Jennifer Ann Daddio

Printed in the United States of America

2   4   6   8   10   9   7   5   3   1

For my brother, Gerald Wayne Hoover, who helped me
with this book and with my life

and

For Rose and Wendell Myers, who made me their
daughter and forgot the in-law

Acknowledgments

THANKS TO MIKE EASTLAND, who is an expert on antique cars, and to Jane Chase, who is an expert on so much.

As usual, I was helped by dear friends. David and Martha Evans did leopard research. Jayne Mays never fails to give helpful suggestions and facts. Marilyn Hoover spends hours proofreading.

My sister, Linnie Howell, always comes through for me in many ways.

Spotting
the
Leopard

I

"I DON'T RECKON HE CAN LIVE," Mama said, and her voice was real low. She straightened up from where she had bent down to examine our old dog Ring. "You two will have to bear it." She looked at Jessie, then at me, and she shook her head. "Won't be easy, but so much of living ain't."

Mama was used to bearing things, but my sister, Jessie, wasn't. "He won't die," she said to me when Mama had left the barn. "We won't let him." She dropped to her knees and stroked his big black head. Ring didn't open his eyes, just went on breathing in that kind of shallow way like the little hold he had on life could slip away at any minute.

We were quiet for a while, staring at Ring's body going up and down with each breath and listening to Bossy chomping hay in her stall. I hunkered down to be beside Jessie and watched her touch our dog over and over. She whispered to him, and I could feel her willing him to live.

1

"Mama says that even an animal doctor couldn't do anything, but there must be something." Jessie jumped up, excited. "H.J., we've got to get that snake!"

"Why?" Jessie had smashed the copperhead's brains with a big rock, and I couldn't imagine what we'd do with the thing.

My sister was pacing back and forth, kicking the straw that covered the barn floor. "I should have remembered right off. In a book I read once the man got bitten by a snake. They cut up the snake's body and used it to press on the bite to draw out the poison."

"Likely just a story, made up and all," I said.

"Maybe. Maybe. But we got to try something." Her hand was on the door latch.

"Wait." I reached out to grab her arm. "You stay here. Keep talking to him." I looked over at Ring. "Maybe he won't die if you keep talking to him."

She went back to drop beside the dog again and smoothed the hairs on his back. "You get the snake," she told me. "Hurry."

Out in the south pasture, I moved fast through the brown grass toward the old cottonwood where Jessie and I had rested on a big fallen limb. Everything had seemed great then. Even though Papa wasn't home, Mama had fixed a baked hen and dressing for Thanksgiving dinner. After the last pan was washed, dried, and put away, I convinced Jessie to go for a walk with me. It was real warm and sunny for November, and I felt good setting out with Ring between us.

It was all my fault. I sucked in my breath and held it, like maybe me not breathing would keep Ring's breaths coming. Of course I had to give up and draw in air, but I ran toward the tree, hard.

The snake was still on the ground beside the limb. Me and Jessie hadn't even noticed him as he coiled silently between us, his red head ready to strike one of us for sure. Ring saw, though, and suddenly he was there fighting the thing. It got him twice on the face and once on the throat before Jessie could heave the big rock.

He was long and fat for a copperhead. Mama said likely that meant he was old and full of poison. Ring was bad sick even before we got home. He wobbled toward the barn ignoring us trying to coax him into the house. He wouldn't touch the water I fetched for him, just looked up at us and whined only once. Then he closed his eyes.

Not wanting to touch the snake, I broke off a little limb from the tree and used it to hook under the long body. But of course I couldn't move fast carrying it like that. I pulled a handkerchief out of my overalls pocket. Without looking at the horrible remains, I grabbed hold and started to run.

Touching the snake didn't trouble Jessie at all. She used my pocket knife to skin it and cut it into hunks.

"Look. Oh look," she said when she held the first piece to the swollen bite on Ring's face. Sure enough, the meat was turning green.

"It's the poison," I whispered in wonder. "It must be drawing out the poison," and I ran to get Mama.

When we got back to the barn, Jessie was holding a piece to the other bite on Ring's face. "Maybe," said Mama. "Just maybe. But don't go counting on anything," she warned.

We were counting, though. We were counting on our dog living. Jessie used every bit of that old snake even after it quit turning green, but Ring never stirred or opened his eyes.

Later Mama brought out blankets. "Knew there wasn't no use in suggesting you two come in to bed," she said, and she patted us as she spread the blankets over our shoulders.

"You might try dabbing on some kerosene," she told us, and she poured some oil into a little bucket before she lit the lamp.

I was glad Mama went back into the house instead of staying with us. Mama liked old Ring, but it was me and Jessie that loved him. It was right for it to be just us beside him in the lamplight. Even if he died, it was right for it to be us.

Jessie kept wetting a cloth in the oil and laying it on the sores. Finally my head and back got so weary that I had to stretch out in the straw. "Just going to rest my eyes," I said. "You yell if anything happens."

She did. Little streaks of light showed through the crack around the barn door when she called out. "H.J."

I was up in a flash, so awful afraid Ring had died while I was sleeping. But he hadn't.

"His eyes are open," Jessie said. "Oh, he's opened his eyes."

I held his mouth while Jessie wet her fingers and let the water drip onto Ring's tongue. He closed his eyes again, but we were both sure he was better.

"I've decided something," Jessie told me. "I'm going to be a veterinarian. You know, take care of animals."

I knew what a being a veterinarian was and there in the dark barn with the smell of manure and kerosene and our dog so terrible sick but likely to get well it seemed possible that my sister could become one.

By the middle of the morning, Ring was holding up his head to lap water from the pan. Jessie and me took turns staying right beside him. Mama gave us the leftover chicken, which we had all lost interest in. We tore it into tiny pieces and rubbed them against his mouth until he ate a little.

He was walking some by the next day when the Dickersons came by to give Jessie a ride back to town with their boy, who also boarded for high school and worked in Mr. Henson's store with Jessie.

"Sure hate to leave Ring," she said when we saw the Dickersons' beat-up Chevrolet coming.

"Just needs to get his strength back," Mama said. "He'll be good as ever, time you come home for Christmas."

I helped Jessie carry her things. Mama was ahead of us and already visiting with Mrs. Dickerson when we got there. "Real nice of you folks to haul Jessie back and forth and all," she said.

Mrs. Dickerson started going on about Jessie being a fine girl, while Mama said nice things about Howard, who jumped out of the backseat. He was sort of grinning all over and was real eager to make sure Jessie and her stuff got settled.

She leaned over to me. "Don't mention my plans," she whispered just before she crawled in the car. "I want to talk to Doc Harris in town. See what all's required."

I nodded my head. If there had been a minute, I'd have asked had she ever heard of a girl vet. In the daylight I doubted such a thing was possible, especially when the girl didn't have one cent for schooling.

The days passed quick. I forgot about Jessie's crazy idea and just enjoyed having Ring beside me again and looked forward to Papa being home for Christmas from his job with the WPA.

By Christmas Eve I was just busting with excitement. I hurried through chores. Even in the rush, though, I threw extra hay in Bossy's trough and took time to put the kicker on her. "Don't you act up now," I said, snapping the little chain on her feet and adding the clasp for her tail. I didn't want her giving me a hoof to the head or a manure slap in the face for Christmas.

Bossy never kicked at Papa or swatted him with her wet, messy tail, but Papa had been gone for a long time. Me and Bossy both missed him.

By the time I finished up and left the barn, one bright star twinkled high over the hill in the north pasture. I stood there with the milk bucket in my hand and looked up in the sky, thinking maybe that was the very star that once marked the stable in Bethlehem, and I said a little thank you to God because Ring was there pressed against my leg.

Good smells from the kitchen hit me even before I stepped inside the house. Mama was bent over the cook table rolling out piecrust, but she looked up when I came in. "Two kinds of pie for dinner tomorrow, son," she said, and she smiled. Back before Papa went off to help build bridges, courthouses, and such for the government, we never would have had two kinds of pie even if it was Christmas.

President Roosevelt thought up the WPA to help folks like our family through hard times, but for me it was awful hard having Papa gone so much. All that evening I kept going to the kitchen window to see if the lights of our old truck might be showing up through the dark.

"Likely he had to wait for Jessie," Mama told me

when I looked out for maybe the third time. "Mr. Henson probably kept her late, not caring about Christmas Eve."

I figured Mama was right. Mr. Henson reminded me of a fellow named Scrooge in a story Mr. Whipple read to us at school. Jessie worked real hard at Henson's Grocery and Dry Goods, but she just barely made enough to cover her room and board with a family in town so that she could go to high school.

Learning stuff meant a whole bunch to Jessie. Talk was going around about how the school in town might start sending buses for high school students even as far out as our place next fall. It aggravated me, them starting buses just when Jessie would be finished up. Our house had been awful lonesome with Jessie and Papa both gone.

The crazy thing was that after all that waiting, a shy spell took hold of me when they finally did come. "They're here," I called out as the lights cut through the night.

"Mercy." Mama wiped the flour off her hands onto her apron, and she smoothed down her hair. I followed her out onto the porch, but I sort of held back as she ran down the steps to meet them.

Papa and Jessie piled out of the truck, laughing and talking at the same time. They had bright packages in their hands. I just stayed on the porch watching Mama hugging at them and Jessie making over Ring. Snow started to fall in fine little flakes, but moonlight filtered through the clouds and sort of lit up Mama, Papa, Jessie, and Ring. To me they looked like a scene on a Christmas card, and I thought I might bust with the gladness filling up my insides.

"Where's H.J.?" Papa shouted, and I went bounding down to take the bag of groceries he had in one arm. He put his big hand on the back of my neck and squeezed. It was something he always did, and the roughness of his callused fingers felt so good to me that I had to swallow hard to keep from tearing up like a baby.

When we got inside, Jessie handed me a package, all wrapped in green paper and tied with a red bow. "I can't wait," she said.

I knew it would be a book. Jessie set a lot of store by books, buying me one for Christmas every year since she went to work at Henson's. She always got to stay home for a few days after Christmas. Evenings we would settle by the fire to read my new book out loud, first Jessie, then me taking a turn.

Mama listened and even Papa did too. Last year it had been *Huckleberry Finn*, so I wasn't surprised at all to take off the paper and see *Tom Sawyer*.

We ended up giving each other all our gifts. Papa had shiny new marbles for me, and Mama brought out a brand-new pouch she'd stitched up from soft red material.

For Jessie I had a little bookcase I'd been working at off and on for a while. It looked pretty good even without Papa there to help me. "I figured you'd need a place for your books when you're done with school and back home," I said.

A sort of funny look showed up in her eyes, and I remembered what she had said that night in the barn about being a veterinarian. I guess I had sort of wanted to forget. I didn't like the idea of my sister going even farther from home or of her heart hurting with wanting to do a thing she just couldn't.

But then she smiled real big and said she loved the bookcase.

Mama rolled the leftover piecrust in sugar with cinnamon and baked it up in the oven. She poured hot cocoa into tin cups, and we had a regular Christmas Eve feast.

When things were quiet, I wiggled down between the quilts on my bed, just feeling good about having Jessie and Papa home and thinking about the good food we'd have for dinner on Christmas.

Jessie stuck her head into my room. "Sleep tight, don't let the bedbugs bite," she said, and she started to move on to her room.

I should have let her go, but instead I called out, "Jessie, wait." She came into my room then and stood at the foot of my bed. "You been thinking still about being a doctor, you know for animals?"

Even in the dim light, her answer was plain before she opened her mouth. She sort of clenched her fists up with excitement. I couldn't see her green eyes, but I knew they were bright as the Christmas tree lights in town. "Yes! Oh yes!" she said. "I've been talking lots to Doc Harris, and he lets me hang around his place some when I've got time."

"That's good, I reckon." What else could I say, her so fired up and all, but a feeling of uneasiness started nudging at the Christmas happiness down inside of me.

When Jessie went on to her room, I rolled over so that I could see the window. The snow was still light, but I decided to study on having a white Christmas. I worked hard at not worrying about Jessie's strange notions.

It came to me to consider what Uncle Delbert might bring me for Christmas. I'd thought about it some since last week.

Buddy was pretty sure his father had bought him something special. We had been talking about the possibilities at Uncle Delbert's Deluxe Tourist Court one day after school, and I had caught Uncle Delbert smiling as he wiped at the restaurant counter.

Buddy noticed the grin too, and he poked me. "Bet he's fixing to buy you a swell present," he whispered when Uncle Delbert went into the kitchen.

"Naw," I said around my bite of lemon meringue

11

pie. "Uncle Delbert's real careful with his money, just getting this tourist court going and all."

I couldn't keep my mind on the gift, though. Finally I went off to sleep counting chickens. They were lots easier for me to picture than sheep.

The next morning I jumped out of bed and went right to the window, not caring about my bare feet on the cold floor. Somehow, I just knew the snow had thickened up in the night, and I was right. It covered everything. Snow was piled on the barn roof and the fence around the cow lot. I could see big footprints leading out to the stock tank, and I knew Papa was already doing chores.

I figured he hadn't called me on account of me doing the work by myself while he was gone. I wanted to just stand there swallowing in how pretty things looked and liking Papa's footprints on our place again, but I also wanted to be out there in the barn with him. I pulled on my clothes as fast as I could.

Mama and Jessie were in the kitchen. I could smell ham cooking, and I could hear them talking. Their words weren't plain, but I figured Jessie was telling about school or about the folks who came into Henson's.

I was wrong, though. I could tell by their tone even before I got all the way into the room. I sort of stopped by the pie safe where they wouldn't notice me, and I listened.

Mama was slicing a loaf of bread. Her face looked sad. "Don't fret so, honey," she said to Jessie.

"I can't help it, Mama. I just can't." There were tears in my sister's eyes.

I was pretty sure what they were discussing, but I said, "What?" before I moved on into the room. "What's going on?"

Neither of them looked at me. I grabbed a hunk of bread and reached for the butter dish.

"Don't eat much," Mama said. "Dinner's early. You'll want to be good and hungry."

Jessie got a saucer and scooped the fat and meat scraps from the cook table where Mama had trimmed the ham. "I'll take these to Ring," she said, and she bolted out the door, not even getting her coat.

I wanted to question Mama, but she bit at her lip like she might take to crying. I got my coat and followed my sister.

Jessie was on the porch with Ring, and he was eating the scraps from her hand. I walked over to them, trying to think what to say. Nothing came out. I reached down and patted Ring.

"Don't worry about me," Jessie said, and she gave me a weak little smile. "I knew Mama was going to say my idea about being a vet was crazy."

"Oh." It was all I could think to say.

13

Jessie hugged herself. "It's cold out here." She turned to go back into the house, but she looked over her shoulder just before she opened the door. "Hey, Merry Christmas." Her smile was bigger this time, but her eyes still looked sad.

I stared after her, with a kind of heaviness growing in my stomach. Shoot, I didn't know a thing about being a veterinarian. Once, back before money got so tight, I could remember Papa had Doc Harris out when Bossy had trouble calving, but that was maybe seven years ago. I was too little to remember much except that I liked his truck. I could see, though, that Jessie was all tore up with wanting to be a vet, and I knew her wanting wouldn't just go away.

I started on out to the barn, trying to walk in Papa's tracks. Folks say me and Jessie both look like Papa with the same red hair and all. Jessie is short like Mama, though. It's me that got Papa's height. He had said just last night that I was about to catch him, but I could see there was a ways to go yet. My legs wouldn't stretch from one of his steps to the other.

Bossy mooed contented like as Papa milked her, and of course he didn't have the kickers on. "Morning," he said when I walked in.

I wanted to talk to him about Jessie, but instead I climbed up on a stall rail and started about the weather.

"Sure did snow. Reckon the roads might be too bad for Uncle Delbert and Aunt Maybell to make it here for dinner?"

"Most likely not. Delbert's got good chains. I'm sort of surprised, him closing the restaurant, though."

"Aunt Maybell wouldn't hear of keeping it open. Said there wouldn't be no one eating in a restaurant on Christmas Day anyways because Christmas is for families."

Papa put the last squeeze on Bossy, stood, and patted her rump. That old cow looked back at him, and I could just about swear she smiled. He went over to pour some of the warm milk into a dish, and Ginger, our yellow barn cat, came a-running.

For a minute I forgot about Jessie. Being in the barn with Papa just felt so good. Over in the opposite stalls, Gee and Haw, our plow horses, munched on their Christmas breakfast. The smell of the leather harnesses that hung on the wall mixed with the smell of manure and hay.

Then it flashed through my mind to wonder why in Sam Hill Jessie would want to leave this place for any reason. But even if I didn't understand it, I knew she did want to, real bad.

"You ever know anyone who went to college?" I asked Papa.

He was heading toward the door, and I got up to follow. "Can't say as I ever did, not personal anyway. Why?" He waited for me, and we went out together.

"Jessie," I said. "She's wanting to be a veterinarian." The breath from our mouths came out like smoke in the cold, but neither of us made a step toward the house. I took the milk bucket while Papa closed the barn door. He moved real slow.

"She told you that, did she?" he asked, like he couldn't believe my words.

I nodded. "Guess she wants it pretty bad."

"There ain't no way." Papa shook his head. "Not no way a-tall, and it ain't even sensible. The girl's getting wild ideas. Reckon I was wrong to let her go on with that high school business."

I thought back to Jessie planning for high school. As I remembered, there wasn't much "letting" to it. My sister could be awful determined when she made up her mind.

Things didn't blow up right off. We went back to the house, and Papa smoked his pipe and read the paper he had brought home from town the night before. "Germany is sure stirring things up over there," he said to me. "Just hope they keep their troubles across the sea and leave us out of it."

Ordinarily, I'd have been real interested in hearing Papa talk about what he read in the paper, but right then

I cared more about what Mama and Jessie were stirring up in the kitchen. My stomach rumbled with hunger, and the smells pulled me over and over into the kitchen, where I'd beg for a bite of sweet taters or swipe a little sliver of ham.

I didn't catch any more talk about college. I did hear Mama say, "Now, Howard Dickerson? You've always been fond of him."

"I don't want to marry anybody, Mama. Not for a long time. I want college and then veterinary school." Jessie walked away from the stove and went over to look out the kitchen window.

"Don't set yourself up for hurt, sugar." Mama's voice sounded tired, and she wiped at a wisp of hair that tumbled out of the bun on the back of her head.

"There won't be no talk of college." Papa was standing in the door. I never did hear him sound so hard before. Papa is an easy kind of man, always careful about how folks feel.

"I'm going," my sister said. "One way or another." She stood absolutely still, and she pulled her lips straight and tight, like she could change it all just by pushing hard on the inside of herself. Right there in a flash, I was on Jessie's side, but I didn't look forward to what Papa would say next.

There was heat in the room, like maybe the fire was about to bust out of the oven.

Just then Uncle Delbert's truck came rattling up to the house. I was sure glad to hurry out to meet them. "Gee whiz," I yelled back into the kitchen, "there's people with them."

Strangers in the house would stop the quarrelsome words between Jessie and Papa, so I was glad to see a woman up in front with Aunt Maybell and Uncle Delbert. Her thin arms were wrapped around a little girl, perched on her lap. A man, all covered up in a quilt, huddled in the back.

Before Uncle Delbert had the motor killed, the kid opened the door to jump out. "Hi, there," she said. "My name's Pearl, and I come to eat Christmas dinner with you." She was a pretty little thing with blond hair, looked to be about seven or so.

Turned out Pearl's papa had come walking up to the Deluxe Tourist Court after his old car gave out in the snow. Aunt Maybell and Uncle Delbert were just loading up to come to our place. They gave Jack Riley a quilt, picked up his wife and child on the way, and now they were all gathering around our table.

"Glad to have neighbors to share our meal with," Papa said, and Mama scurried around setting three more plates.

Mr. Riley kept repeating, "Much obliged," every time a bowl was passed to him.

"We was trying to make it to Tulsa," his wife explained. "There ain't been no work for the longest, but we got people in Tulsa."

"Family," said Uncle Delbert. "It's sure nice to be near kin, especially when a helping hand's needed." He took the bread platter from Jessie.

Right then the idea struck me harder than the barn door on a windy day. Maybe Uncle Delbert might see his way clear to help Jessie go to college.

I knew Papa had been against Uncle Delbert and Aunt Maybell selling the land that used to be Grandpa's so they could build the Deluxe Tourist Court.

"Delbert's too much of a dreamer," Papa had said. "Land, that's what you got to hold on to even when times is bad."

Still, the tourist business seemed to be doing pretty good. They had five neat white cabins. Lots of days after school I'd go over there for an orange soda pop or a piece of pie, and I had noticed that the cabins usually had somebody in them. Aunt Maybell cooked up mighty fine food at the restaurant, too, and word was getting around to the men who hauled stuff up and down Highway 66.

Before I could finish the thought, Mama poked me. "H.J.," she said. "Stop setting there holding that gravy bowl like you was asleep and hand it on to little Pearl."

"Oh, sure." I passed the gravy, even dished it out for the girl, but all through dinner I'd look over at Uncle Delbert and wonder his opinion about girls and college.

I hadn't quite finished my pumpkin pie when Uncle Delbert got up. There was a big grin on his face. "I'll be right back," he said. "We got presents in the truck."

I scooted my saucer of pie away and watched him go out the kitchen door. That present had got to be real important to me. My mind was made up. If Uncle Delbert came back in with an expensive gift for me, I'd take it as a sign that things were easing up for him. I'd wait for a chance to ask him about helping Jessie. I put my fork down and looked over at Papa, wondering how he'd take to Uncle Delbert giving Jessie the money. Papa wasn't one for being beholden to folks. It was most usually him that did the giving.

The door behind me slammed, and I knew Uncle Delbert was back. Holding my breath, I didn't turn around until he said, "H.J."

He held out a good-sized box, and I stood up to take it. Just one piece of tape held the box closed, but I didn't tear in right off. Instead I looked up at Papa. His eyes had a little shadow of sadness in them, and it came to me that Papa would have liked to buy me something more than marbles for Christmas.

"Go ahead, boy. Open it," Uncle Delbert said, but I was still watching Papa. He nodded his head, and I tore off the end of the box with the tape, sucking in my breath from surprise as I saw the smooth leather ball mitt and the bright new ball.

"There's a bat, too," said Uncle Delbert. He opened the front door and reached out to lift in a brand-new bat.

"Golly," I said. "Thanks." I had looked often at ball mitts in Mr. Henson's store. They sure weren't cheap.

There was a box for Jessie, too. "I ordered from the wish book," Aunt Maybell said when Jessie took out two bolts of dress goods. "Wanted something you didn't handle every day at Henson's."

"I'll make up the corduroy right away, and save the flowers for spring." Jessie unrolled some of the bright cloth and talked about how pretty it was. She smiled real big, but I could still see the misery about college beneath the smile.

Right away, though, my mind shot from Jessie to Pearl, across from me at the table. There she was, a little girl with not one toy on Christmas. She leaned against her mama, who stroked her hair.

Maybe I could go get my marbles or my book for her. I didn't figure a girl would be real taken with the marbles, but she might like them better than a book, which she was likely too little to read.

Just then something made me glance up to see Mama. She stood in the doorway, and she held Mary Beth, the doll that used to belong to my little sister, Patsy, before she died. With one hand Mama held the rag doll out to Pearl. With the other hand she smoothed the dress on Mary Beth's soft body. "Look what Santy Claus left for Pearl," Mama said.

A little gasp came from someone at the table, likely Aunt Maybell or Jessie. We all knew how special that doll was to Mama. Patsy died six years ago, when I was just about ready to start school, but that awful time stuck permanent in my mind. I remembered how Mama thought to put the doll in the box with Patsy, but how she had changed her mind and kept the only thing she had left of her little girl.

It was Papa everybody worried about most because he sort of gave up for a while when Patsy died, but what I saw Mama doing once was the plainest in my mind. Late at night after things had just about got back to normal, I got up from bed to creep into the kitchen for a drink of water from the bucket. Through the doorway I saw Mama in the front room. She was in Grandma's old chair, rocking Mary Beth and singing real soft.

Pearl jumped up, hopped right over the bench she had been on at the table, and ran to Mama. "For me?" Her face was as bright as the sun on the snow outside.

"Yes." Mama laid Mary Beth up against her cheek one last time, then put her in the little outstretched hand. "Ole Santy Claus, he said it was time Mary Beth belonged to you."

Pearl took that doll and went to loving it right off. "I've got some pretty scraps, just big enough to make that baby a nice new dress," Aunt Maybell said, and she wiped at her eyes.

There was sadness around that Christmas table with us, but there was gladness too. I had a thought that good things sort of waited for us in the new year.

I felt all full of Christmas, and I wanted to do something for my sister. "Jessie's got a terrible yearning to go on to school," I blurted out. "College. Will you help her, Uncle Delbert?"

The room got real quiet except for Pearl, who was cradling Mary Beth and talking to her in a little soft voice.

Aunt Maybell made a sort of nervous, clearing-her-throat kind of sound. Then she said, "Well, now, that's something to think about, ain't it, Delbert?" She leaned across the table toward him.

He shook his head. "No, Maybell, there just ain't no use to get the girl's hopes up. We ain't got that kind of money, the business is too young. Seems like, though, the restaurant is real up and coming." His face sort of brightened. "Might be we could hire Jessie on part-time to help Maybell cook come next fall."

Jessie made a noise like the wind was just knocked out of her, and Papa reached across me to put his hand over hers where she was gripping tight to the edge of her plate.

"There ain't nothing important to me and your mama

except you and your brother," he said. "Lord knows I'd give you the money if I had it even if it does seem like new-fangled nonsense to me. But it can't be. The WPA work's fixing to play out. I'm struggling hard to set aside a few dollars for another cow, hoping to build up a little dairy."

Jessie jumped up over the bench and started grabbing up dirty dishes. "Uncle Delbert," she said, "I'm sorry H.J. said anything. I know you're working hard to get your place going. I wouldn't consider taking your money even if you offered it." Then she turned and looked right at Papa. "I'm going to college, though. I know I can get a job there for some of the money, and I'll get the rest of it somehow."

That's when Papa shot off his chair. "Got to check the stock," he muttered, and with his head down he made for the door.

Jessie smiled real big and kept stacking dishes. "I will go," she said to Papa's back. Her voice was soft, but it's like there's this string or wire or something strung between my guts and my sister's. I knew none of the fire had gone out of her. I knew too that out in the barn Papa was storming around, maybe even kicking at the cat. We're headed for hard times, I thought. Real hard times.

2

THE REST OF CHRISTMAS vacation didn't turn out to be much fun either. Jessie started to read *Tom Sawyer* with me, but she didn't even smile at the funny parts. The second night I didn't bring up the book, and neither did she. Instead she went outside and set right down on the front-porch chair like it was summer.

When I went out there, she was staring up at the sky. "The stars seem brighter in winter," she said. "But I don't know if they really are or not. I've got to learn things." She shrugged her shoulders like it was a hopeless question.

I started to say I'd ask Mr. Whipple at school or that surely one of her high school teachers would know, but I could see there was more, that just knowing the one answer wouldn't really soothe her none.

Ring came up and put his head in Jessie's lap. "I'll tell you both something right now," she said. She petted Ring's head, but it was me she looked at. "I'm going to college. Papa may not see a way or the need. Uncle Delbert may never give me a penny, but I'm going."

"I'll help you," I said. I didn't have even one idea about how I could do it, but it was a promise I had to make.

The first thing that come to me was that I would take the ball, mitt, and bat back. I slipped the mitt and ball back into the box. I loved that present, the best one I'd ever got, but I reminded myself of how Mama gave Patsy's doll to that little girl.

Papa was working closer now. He got to come home one Saturday not long after Christmas, and I went to town with him. "I'm taking it back," I told him when I climbed into the truck with the stuff. "Going to give the money to Jessie for college."

He made a kind of snorting noise that reminded me of a bull not wanting to go into a dipping vat to get rid of ticks. "Your sister is too stubborn to give up yet," he said, "but I wish you wouldn't egg her on."

It didn't seem like Jessie needed any encouraging. "I guess you'll have to get lots more," I said when I gave her the money.

She just tucked the fifteen dollars into the drawer of our old chiffonier, and she smiled. "The rest will come," she said.

I tried to smile back at her, but Papa was stomping around the front room shouting about how he could not find his newspaper. I worried about Jessie and I worried about Papa.

Nothing much happened all winter. Every time Jessie was able to make it home, it seemed like there was a kind of tightness about her like her eyes were darting for a way out, and she had to keep her body ready to jump in case she saw it.

The first real day of spring something good did happen, and me and Buddy had the most fun we'd had in a coon's age. We were walking along home from school just talking about how Mr. Whipple had busted our behinds for not finishing our arithmetic. We started counting up how many paddlings we'd had since September. Buddy thought he'd had more, but I was pretty sure it was me held the record.

"Think we ought to take to calling him the Whipper," Buddy said.

"Yeah, and his first name is Ernest. Ernest Whipper. It sure fits."

We were still cracking jokes about the teacher's name when we heard a noise. It was the Cansters and their old black truck with the back full of little Cansters. Joe Tom, the same age as me and Buddy but still in the primary class, and Robert, who quit before he finished eighth grade, was up in front with their father. None of the Canster bunch had been in school that day, and we found out why.

Dust swirled around us as the truck came to a rattling stop while the engine gave a sort of cough. Mr. Canster stuck his head out the window. "You boys seen a stray heifer?" he asked. "We spent pretty nigh all day looking for her, a real pretty jersey. Got a white streak down her face. Her name's Susie."

Buddy looked over at me, wondering what I'd say. He figured I wouldn't be much interested in helping with any Canster troubles because Jessie and me were pretty sure it was Mr. Canster who put a bullet in Ring's leg when he was just a young dog. Mr. Canster claimed our dog was after cattle.

Still, it wasn't a lie when I spoke up and said, "We ain't seen her." The thing was, though, that their truck was just barely out of sight when we did. There she was, wandering across the road not thirty yards in front of us.

"Susie? Don't you reckon?" I asked.

"Ain't that the name of one of them scrawny Canster girls?" Buddy asked. He was grinning real big.

"Crazy old man probably don't know the difference." A wonderful idea was growing in my head. I started unbuttoning my shirt.

"What you doing?"

"We got to use this shirt for a rope," I said, "and yours too."

"Huh?" he asked, but he started taking his off.

"You think Mr. Whipple is gone from school yet?"

Buddy's grin got even bigger. "We fooled around the river for a good bit of time."

"Well," I announced with pride, "if we can find a way in, maybe through a window, Miss Susie Canster is going to get her a little education."

Buddy wiggled with pleasure. "It's high time she had some learning."

Finding the window to crawl through and unlocking the front door was easy. Convincing Susie was not. We pushed and pulled and coaxed. I was on the wrong end of the cow when she decided to let go. I was bent over her rear end pushing and the squirted manure just missed my face and covered my boots. Buddy almost fell over laughing.

Finally we shoved Susie through the front door and slammed it. "Seems to me," I told Buddy while I was wiping my boots on the grass, "that I've heard a real interesting fact about cows. Sometimes you can shove them up stairs, but you can't ever shove them back down."

All the work was worth it because my prophesy came true. The next morning all of us kids watched while Mr. Whipple worked on that heifer.

Two eighth-grade boys tried to help, pushing and pleading. Mr. Whipple was red in the face. "I demand you come down here at once," he thundered, and he shook his finger at sweet Susie, who only wanted to learn. But he had to stop pointing and grab his pants because his belt was being used for a rope.

In the end, we got a little vacation, which was just great on the second really warm day of spring. Me and Buddy spent the day fishing and laughing about how Mr. Canster backed his truck right up to the school steps, and they lifted poor Susie, bawling and kicking her protest, into the back. Not wanting anyone to notice us and think maybe the cow hadn't wandered in through a door left accidentally open, we headed out for the river instead of staying around to help with the cleanup.

I needed all the fun I could get at school. Things at home were pretty black. Papa, when he was there, was riled about half the time over Jessie and her college talk.

"I've got an idea," she told me one weekend when she'd caught a ride home with Buddy's father. She spread out a big catalog on the kitchen table. "See," she told me. "I'm going to be an agent for Montgomery Ward's."

She had some forms with her name stamped on them, and she was supposed to get folks to order from the catalog. Then the company would send her some percent of the money.

Jessie worked real hard at the catalog business, walked all over town knocking on doors after she got off from working for Mr. Henson, but when she came home next time she had only added two orders to the one Aunt Maybell had given her right off.

"Three dollars ain't going to pay your college bills,"

Papa thundered. I hadn't ever seen him so mad at Jessie. He was mad at Aunt Maybell too. "Shouldn't be encouraging the girl to work her heart out for an impossible aim," he said. "Seems to me Delbert is dream chaser enough to have in one family." He slammed out the door and went to chop kindling, even though the wood box was full.

Jessie didn't say a word, just folded her arms across her chest and stared after him.

"Your papa loves you, Jessie," Mama said. "He's a prideful man, and deep down it hurts him that he can't do for you what you want so much."

Jessie bit her lip and never said a word about giving up.

Finally toward the end of March, the second good thing happened. Uncle Delbert had to drive up to the city because the hot water tank in one of the cabins went bust. He was real proud of having a modern bathroom in each cabin with a stool that flushed and enough hot water for two baths.

All the bathroom fixtures had been delivered from a company in the city, and he figured he could get them to make good if he took back the busted tank.

Papa was working with the WPA again at Lincoln Park Zoo, and Uncle Delbert dropped me off there to see Papa and walk around the zoo. He gave me money for a snow cone and two hot dogs.

"I could of give you some pocket money," Papa said when I saw him. It seemed to me he should just be glad Uncle Delbert brought me, but Papa was near about as put out with Delbert lately as he was with Jessie. I figured it was because he had made such a fuss about Delbert selling the land, and now it looked like Papa had been wrong. Papa and Uncle Delbert didn't have much to say to each other. They didn't even argue about politics anymore.

Papa couldn't take off from working on the zoo train track to go around with me much, but we did get to see the big cats together. There was a striped tiger, and two big lions, asleep in the sun, but it was the leopard I looked at most.

I can't say as I really liked looking at Lucky, which the sign said was his name, but I couldn't not look at him either.

He was down in a deep stone pit. I leaned on the log rail and watched that leopard pace back and forth, back and forth. Once he stopped and looked right at me with his yellow eyes. Misery just plain dripped from that animal.

"He's new," Papa said. "They just bought him." He shook his head and put his hand on my shoulder. "I know how he feels, son. I've been up against it more than once my own self."

"I think Jessie's feeling the same way," I said.

"I know." Papa's voice was real soft.

We just stayed there until Papa had to go back to work, both of us leaning on those rails and both of us thinking. Those few minutes with Papa meant more to me than seeing the animals or eating the snow cone and hot dogs.

After he left, I went on to some other animals, but I came back twice to look at Lucky. I wished he would just give up and rest in the sun like the lions, and I finally understood why Papa was so mad at Jessie. He wanted her to do the same thing.

3

WHEN I GOT HOME from the zoo, I told Mama all about
seeing Papa, and about the food, and about all the other
animals. I didn't say a word about Lucky. The picture of
that big cat was real fresh in my mind, and I just did not
feel like talking about him.

The really crazy thing was that in just a few days
everybody was talking about Lucky. It started with
Buddy. I could see by the way he motioned for me to
hurry as I walked toward him that he was excited about
something. There sure wasn't any chance he was fired up
about going to school.

There wasn't nothing Buddy wouldn't do to get out
of school. Last spring he found a litter of new-born
skunks, and it beat all how at least once a week he would
make a visit to that skunk nursery just to rile the mama.
By the time I came along he was already sprayed. I didn't
walk close to Buddy, but he didn't care because he knew
he would get sent home as soon as school started.

"You most certainly are an unfortunate young man,

Hiram," Mr. Whipple would say, turning toward the door for air. Mr. Whipple never called us H.J. and Buddy because he did not believe in nicknames. "Home," the teacher would say. Buddy always dropped his eyes and nodded his head mournfully, but I knew he'd dance as soon as he got out of the schoolhouse, and in no time at all he'd have his fishing pole, heading for the river.

So, from the way Buddy was hurrying me, I sort of figured he had come up with another good hooky scheme. He hadn't, though. He was excited about Lucky.

"Guess what," he yelled. "Some great big cat's busted out of the zoo in Oklahoma City."

I stopped like somebody had yanked my harness, and right then I knew it wasn't the striped tiger or either of them big lions. If there really was a cat loose from Lincoln Park Zoo, it had to be Lucky. I reckon I was on the side of that animal right from the start because my heart went to racing. Buddy came toward me grinning.

"How you know?" I asked when he was close.

"Heard it on the radio. Ain't it something? They're all worked up over it in the city, got lots of folks out looking. I expect your papa's hunting that leopard."

"It was Lucky, then?"

Buddy laughed. "Sounds like you're personal acquainted with that cat. You have supper with him or something up to the zoo?"

36

I shook my head. "I seen him." I didn't even try to explain how watching that cat had made me feel. I didn't have the words.

"So you reckon your papa's in on the chase?"

I shook my head again. "He's up in Tulsa now. Come through the other night, left the truck, and rode on with one of the other fellows."

Buddy reached out and grabbed my arm. "I got it! Let's go back to your place, get the truck, drive up to the city, and volunteer to help find that cat."

"You ain't serious? Nobody but Papa can make that old truck hold together for such a long trip. Anyway, in towns they got laws about kids driving."

"Don't get all in a lather. I was just dreaming, but it sure would be fun. Hey, we better head on to school."

We started walking, but I watched Buddy's face. "Never have seen you in a hurry to get to school."

He grinned sort of sheepish. "Well, I got an idea. I'm thinking we get to Jewel Tea's just about when she's setting out, tell her about the leopard."

"Why?"

Jewel Tea was the other sixth grader at our school. Since first grade, me and Buddy had been aggravating her every chance we got, and Buddy had a plan. "We could scare her about the cat. Make her think it might get her."

I didn't like the idea of using Lucky that way, but not knowing how to say, so I just nodded.

She was just coming out of her big white house when we got there. Jewel Tea lives with her grandma and grandpa. Sometimes she gets letters from her mama, who is off in California. She never did mention a father.

Her name was on account of the man who sold tea and spices for the Jewel Tea Company. He was at the house when she decided to get born. There was no time to send for the doctor, and instead of making a sale, the salesman had to see to the birthing. They let the salesman name the baby, likely to make up for the lost business. Anyway, that story was about the only thing I found interesting about Jewel Tea.

"You hear about the escaped leopard?" Buddy asked as soon as we got up to her.

"I heard," she said, "but I ain't wanting to have a conversation with you two. I'm wanting to walk to school in peace. I declare, there are times some people just plain get on a person's nerves." She sort of squinted up her nose and shook her head hard.

"Well," Buddy paused to kick at a clod of red dirt, "reckon you can walk back there by yourself if you're a mind to. I just hope we don't get out of earshot on account of the leopard."

Buddy looked over at me, wanting me to play along.

"That's right," I said. "We figure that leopard's just about here by now."

Jewel Tea glanced back and forth at the trees on both sides of the road. "It wouldn't of come this far."

I sort of yawned and stretched. "Oh, I don't know. Papa worked down at the zoo, you know, for the WPA, helped build the very pit that leopard jumped out of. He figures that's pretty much exactly what a cat like that'd do, just take to the river, stay right beside it all the way. Wouldn't need no time to get here."

"You really think it could have come all the way from the city? It ain't been out long."

I shook my head indicating a solemn yes, and for a minute she was about to believe me, but then her lips formed a disgusted frown. "H.J. Harper, you ain't even been talking to your papa about that cat. He's not even at home. Ain't that so?"

"H.J. was up there with his papa," Buddy said real quick. Then he bent down to pull at a clump of sheep sorrel that was growing by the side of the road and grabbed a green piece to chew on, stalling for time to think before he said more. "They talked about leopards plenty. They're a real particular interest of H.J.'s."

It was not a lie. "Me and Papa talked about that leopard all right." A picture of the cat pacing in his cage came to me. "They'll never catch him," I said.

39

I guess my voice sounded real truthful because she stayed right beside us all the way to school, half trotting if we moved too fast. Every once in a while Buddy or me would stop real sudden and glance off to the side of the road with a "What's that?" or a "Did you see something move?"

"You don't reckon it's true?" Buddy questioned when we had reached the school ground and Jewel Tea had gone off to tell her fears to the other girls. "That leopard wouldn't really make it this far?"

"Shoot no. But it's fun to see her squirm." I bent down to pick up a piece of sandstone and heaved it off into the trees. I wanted to tell Buddy about how Lucky looked, wanted to make him understand that I was on the leopard's side, but I couldn't.

Mr. Whipple put us to reading about the Civil War right off. Usually, I'm real taken with that part of history, but I couldn't get my mind on it all. I guess I wasn't the only one because Jewel Tea stuck up her hand. "Mr. Whipple," she said right out loud when he kept working with the little kids and didn't notice her. "Do you reckon it is true that leopard's hiding around the school some place?"

I think maybe it wasn't the first time Mr. Whipple had heard the question. "I do not," he said, and his voice sounded aggravated. "Undoubtedly that cat is still in the city area and may well have been recaptured by this time."

I bit my lip, hating the part about Lucky being caught.

All day I kept thinking about the cat and wondering what was going on with him. I figured Aunt Maybell and Uncle Delbert had heard talk about the escape from folks in the restaurant, and on the way home I told Buddy I was cutting over to the highway.

We made frequent detours to the Deluxe Tourist Court on our way home from school. Uncle Delbert would pull two orange soda pops, dripping ice and wet with fog, from the red metal box. Usually Aunt Maybell had a couple of extra pieces of pie. Lemon meringue was my personal favorite.

This time, though, Buddy shook his head. "Can't. Promised my daddy I'd work on the fence some before dark." I was glad, not really wanting company.

"See ya." I cut off through the Johnson grass. I sure liked walking across country in the springtime. Before long roasting ears and watermelon would be growing, and I'd have all summer out of school. The thought made me stop short, but not to look at the trees all green and full. I swallowed hard. What was Jessie going to do? If she had to come home and help Aunt Maybell in the restaurant, she was going to be as miserable as Lucky in his cage.

I forgot about Jessie and Lucky, though, when I saw the Cadillac. It stood square in front of cabin 3 and the red lacquered fenders were brighter than the neon sign Uncle Delbert always turned on way before dark.

I stopped back on the gravel driveway, but that car pulled me. I sort of inched onto the grass in its direction. My hand was out, wanting to touch the shine, but I knew I shouldn't. Maybe, though, I'd get close enough to see my reflection in the curve of the fender. I glanced toward the cabin. No one moved near the door or lifted the green-checkered curtain to look out.

I went right over to the Cadillac. I could see now that the window was down. It would be easy to slip up onto the running board, and I did. Why shouldn't I lean in for one quick grip on the steering wheel?

I looked over my shoulder. Uncle Delbert wouldn't want me messing with a customer's car. He called the people who stayed in his cabins "clientele," and he was always rushing to get one a road map or to help another one fix a flat.

Still, a fast look wouldn't hurt a thing. Especially if no one saw me. I checked cabin 3 again. All clear.

My head was in. I didn't plan on reaching for that horn, but suddenly the smell, the touch was not enough. I had to hear that sound. My hand shot out to push the shiny metal.

For a second I was lost in the beautiful rhythm of the horn. I forgot all about the Deluxe Tourist Court and how Uncle Delbert hustled to please the clientele.

Thrilled with the melody, I hit the horn ring one more time.

"Whoa now, boy. Don't be using up all the electrical juice."

I whirled around. A big man had come from the restaurant. He held the jacket of his pinstriped suit draped over one shoulder. He puffed on a huge cigar, and he waved a giant straw hat at me.

He'll wallop me, I thought, and I stiffened, waiting, but he didn't seem to be in no hurry, just lumbered toward me. I noticed the flash of a shiny ring on his finger. Then I saw he was smiling.

"Want to set in her?" he called. "Go ahead. Open her up and climb on in."

I guess that's when I started to admire the man I would come to know as Ralph Summers. There was so much to admire about him. I admired his Cadillac. And I admired his willingness to let me admire it. In many ways Mr. Ralph Summers was the biggest man I had ever seen.

With my fingers on the handle, I looked back at him once more. He nodded his great gray head. "Get on in if you've a mind to."

I did. He went around to the passenger's side, opened the door, and took the seat beside me. The Cadillac sort of squeaked and gave with his weight, and the smoke from his cigar mixed with the new smell of the car.

"Want to start her up, son?" he asked, and he held out the gleaming key.

Excitement made my hand shake. I had started Papa's old truck for years, had driven it around the fields and country roads plenty. But to start the Cadillac!

Sitting there, I felt like a sure-enough big shot. My imagination started working. What if this man said, "Want to take her for a spin, son?" What if folks saw me driving that car? Boy, wait till Buddy heard about this.

My daydream was interrupted. "H.J., you get out of that automobile." It was my aunt Maybell's voice. She stood by the car, wiping her hands on her apron.

Uncle Delbert hurried up behind her and said something I couldn't hear over the sound of the engine. Aunt Maybell shook her head no, and her face started to turn red. "I said get out, H.J.," she shouted.

Aunt Maybell had never yelled at me, not in my whole life, so I moved quick. Mr. Summers got out of his side and sort of leaned across the red car toward where I stood with my aunt and uncle. "No harm intended. I wasn't fixing to kidnap the boy." He flashed a big smile.

Uncle Delbert let go a loud laugh. "Shoot, no, Ralph. Course you wasn't. Course not."

Aunt Maybell didn't say a word, just reached out and took hold of my arm. Her hand was still damp from the dishpan, and the smell of fried chicken clung to her hair and clothes. Something else clung to her, something I wasn't used to with my aunt. There was anger, but I was pretty sure fear was there too. I looked close at her, but I could tell not to ask questions.

"You go on in." She motioned toward the restaurant and the living quarters behind it. "Today's paper's on the counter. You can read about that cat, escaped from the zoo."

I sort of hesitated. Uncle Delbert looked like he wanted to protest. "Real treat for the boy," he muttered softly, "seeing an automobile fine as this one."

"He's my brother's child," snapped Aunt Maybell, "and I say I don't want him in that car."

Her hands were on her hips, and she was tapping her foot up and down like she heard some army music. I didn't argue, just headed for the restaurant.

"Get yourself a soda pop," Uncle Delbert called after me.

"And a piece of pie," added Aunt Maybell. "You're welcome to anything you see in the kitchen." Her voice was easier, and I knew it wasn't me she was mad at.

Inside the restaurant, I watched out the window. Aunt Maybell stomped off toward the little wash house where she did the motel laundry. Uncle Delbert sort of trotted alongside her for a minute, talking and waving his hands. She didn't appear to say much, just kept right on walking, her face set in hard lines.

Finally Uncle Delbert shrugged and let her go on

without him. He turned back and went over to where two cane-bottom chairs waited under the big cotton-wood out by the drive. Mr. Summers had settled on one, and he waved at Uncle Delbert to join him. Right off the two of them fell to talking hard. Every once in a while Mr. Summers would reach over and slap at Uncle Delbert's back, and I could see them laugh.

I walked away from the window, thinking. Mr. Summers sure seemed like a nice fellow to me, but I could imagine Aunt Maybell in the wash house tossing the sheets into her big tin washtub and stirring them hard with the stick. From the way she had acted, it was pretty clear she didn't like Mr. Summers one little bit. I figured she was wishing she could run him through the big wringer. I sure wondered why.

There was a round plastic display case on the end of the linoleum-covered counter, and it was full of lemon meringue pie, already cut in big slices and resting on saucers. I got a fork from the stack under the counter and settled myself on a round stool.

The newspaper was right beside me. I hadn't even swallowed the first bite when I saw the picture. I kept eating the pie, but the sweet, smooth taste was wasted on me. I was lost in Lucky the leopard, lost in his picture and in his story.

He was called Lucky, the story said, because he had been found as a cub, wandering on a plain in India, orphaned, and half dead. He was lucky, they claimed, to be alive and lucky to be sold when he grew up to so fine a zoo as the one in Oklahoma City.

But I knew Lucky wasn't happy in his new home, and he took a mighty leap, just jumped out of his eighteen-foot-deep pit, landed for a minute on the log railing, and then he was gone.

Everyone was awful excited about the cat roaming around. A man named Mr. Andrews, who was Lucky's keeper, talked about how humans were not in a lot of danger since leopards usually attack small creatures, but he said they are ferocious animals and caution should be used. But the main thing was that he wanted to plead with folks not to shoot Lucky unless absolutely necessary.

There was lots more. In fact the whole *Daily Oklahoman* was full of the escape, how some dogs that are especially trained to hunt big cats had got flown in from Colorado, and about how a calf was found killed north of the city, but how it might not have been Lucky's work at all.

When I was finished with the story, I stayed on the stool licking my lips, letting the pie settle in my stomach, and letting Lucky fill my mind. I could imagine the big cat, moving out of the city at night. In my mind I saw him tense up when some dogs barked at him. I could picture the muscles in his great shoulders growing tight as he stood sort of sniffing the air. He would be afraid out there, but he would also be free.

Uncle Delbert and Mr. Summers had completely gone out of my mind until the front door slammed and my uncle came in. Through the window, I could see Mr. Summers going to his cabin.

"That's some car," I said to Uncle Delbert.

He tried to smile at me, but his heart just wasn't in it. "Dang woman." He got a wet towel and wiped at the restaurant counter, which was already clean. Aunt Maybell and Uncle Delbert kept the Deluxe Tourist Court absolutely spotless.

For a while I watched Uncle Delbert, who kept dipping his cloth in a pan of water and scrubbing on the counter.

"What's Aunt Maybell all fired up about?" I asked when he finally stopped cleaning and leaned on his elbow.

"There ain't a better woman in the whole United States of America than your aunt, H.J.," he said, but he shook his head. "She's got one major fault, though. The woman ain't got no vision. Not one iota of vision."

He tossed the towel on a shelf and headed toward the door. "A body's got to have vision, son," he added just before going out. "Without vision you ain't got a thing."

I watched him head over to the wash house. Then I put my empty soda pop bottle in the crate where it would get counted by the delivery man, who would deduct a penny from Uncle Delbert's bill on account of the returned empty. I carried my saucer and fork back to the kitchen and washed them in the dishpan where Aunt Maybell's water was still warm.

It was tempting to hang around until my aunt and uncle came back in. I sure wanted to know what was going on, but it seemed like they might not be in the mood for company. Besides, I knew Mama would be looking for me to show up at home any time now.

Just when I started off, a car drove in, more of Uncle Delbert's clientele. I stopped at the edge of the drive, moved onto the grass, and watched the family for a minute.

The car wasn't fancy at all, sort of a beat-up Ford with a Texas tag, but the man and woman who got out looked happy and the three little girls were laughing. One of the girls reminded me of little Pearl, whose mama had sent us a postcard from Tulsa. This mother took out a wicker basket and started spreading a blue cloth for a picnic in front of cabin 4. It was a real pretty picture with the Deluxe Tourist Court and Uncle Delbert smiling in the background.

I was hotfooting it across the pasture toward home when I saw something else, something that didn't make me feel good. That land was familiar, belonging to my family like it did.

Every morning after I milked, I'd let Bossy out into that pasture. Every evening, I'd come out and drive her in. Like I said, I knew every hole and rock. It wasn't one bit necessary for me to stop and look around me, but suddenly I did.

Something was different. I didn't know what, but I could feel it.

I stood still, scratched my head, and looked. I was on a grassy little hill and over to the right were some trees.

Something sort of pulled me in that direction. I moved into the woods to a little clearing where a huge cottonwood grew down by a tiny stream.

Sand was piled up under the tree. An animal had been there, stretched out. Its outline was easy to see, something big, but not as big as a cow. Grass grew where the feet had rested, so there wasn't a sign of tracks.

I bent down and traced the shape in the warm sand. "Ring," I said, and the sound of my voice sort of calmed me. "Ring was out here, I guess." But the more I looked the more I doubted it. The outline was awful big for Ring to have made. Besides, he stayed real close to home unless he was with one of the family.

"Just take to the river," I had told Jewel Tea about the leopard. "Wouldn't take no time to get here."

I started to run, but then I stopped. What was I going to do? Go busting in yelling to Mama that the leopard had been in our pasture? It'd scare her to death. She wouldn't let me stir outside till the cat was captured.

Anyway, the whole thing was crazy. I just had the jitters. Hadn't the paper said people were jumpy? One man had claimed to see the leopard chasing his horses, but it turned out to be his neighbor's dog.

No need to go around making far-fetched claims. The rest of the way home, I stayed away from the trees and turned my head after almost every step to look back over my shoulder.

"I'm real tired," I told Mama not long after supper. She had her mending basket out and was settling near the radio to listen to "Fibber McGee and Molly."

I was tired, worn out from thinking about the leopard and wondering what was going on at the Deluxe Tourist Court, but I couldn't sleep.

Down by the barn an owl hooted out into the night, and the sound mixed with the radio voices from the front room. A lonesome feeling started filling me up.

I took to wishing Papa was home. He'd be out on the porch with his pipe just soaking in the night noises. I'd go out and sprawl across the top step. It would be easy to talk to Papa about the leopard. He had a special appreciation of what nature made—deer, birds, and even rocks. He called them "blessed gifts."

Papa would understand how I felt about Lucky. He'd know what to say to make me easier inside. Papa wasn't home, though.

For a minute I thought of going in to be near Mama.

I didn't want to say anything about the cat, but it might be nice just to be close by her. She'd be sure to pat my shoulder and say she was proud of how I was taking hold around the place with Papa gone.

It would make me seem like a baby, though, running to my mama. I rolled over next to the window. "Ring," I called, real soft. "Here, boy."

In the moonlight I could see him bounding across the yard, and then he whined beneath my window. "Good dog," I said, and I rested my arm on the sill. The lonesome feeling went away some. Finally, I fell asleep.

4

NEXT MORNING I padded in to breakfast barefoot. It was, I figured, warm enough to go to school without my winter shoes. Mama stood at the stove, and I could smell eggs.

While she cooked, I made up my mind to tell her about what had gone on at the tourist court. "There was a fellow over at Uncle Delbert's yesterday. Had a real fancy Cadillac. He sure seemed like a mighty nice man, allowed me to set in his car and all, but Aunt Maybell didn't like him. Wouldn't let me hang around none. Him and Uncle Delbert really hit it off, though."

Mama was interested. She brought her coffee to the table and settled down across from me. "Was the fellow selling cars, you think?"

I shrugged my shoulders.

Mama sipped at her coffee. "Maybell's been fretting on Delbert getting high-flown ideas. Says he's not used to money in his pocket. Maybe she's afraid he'll haul off and buy an expensive automobile."

I grinned. "That one was sure a beauty," I said around a mouthful of egg.

"H.J. Harper, don't talk with your mouth full, and don't you go carrying on about that car to Delbert, either. The man's plain soft when it comes to you. He's liable to go out and buy a flashy machine just to please you."

I shook my head. "No, I reckon if Uncle Delbert would do something like that just on my say-so, he'd give Jessie money for college. I asked him again when I told him about taking back the mitt and stuff."

Mama rested her face in her hands for just a second. "It's a worry, seeing Jessie strain so. Almost dread her coming home tonight." She looked up at me. "Don't keep after Delbert, though. It'd be too much of a burden on him, likely take every spare penny he could have. Besides, I don't know as your papa'd allow his help."

She got up and went back to the stove to get her some eggs, and as she walked she changed the subject. "Fellows on the radio are right fired up about that cat escaped from the zoo."

My throat sort of filled up, but it wasn't with food. It was with the same feeling I first had when I saw Lucky down in his concrete pit. I hated seeing trapped things, like my sister and that cat.

Mama turned from the stove and seemed to expect some response, so I managed a nod.

She brought her breakfast back to the table. "I don't reckon one of them things would travel this far. But lands, there ain't no telling. Sure hope your papa makes it home soon."

I wanted him home too but didn't let on. "They'll find that leopard soon, I bet. They got special dogs and everything." I intended to make Mama feel better, and she smiled. My words sure didn't do much for my own feelings, though.

I stared down at the eggs on my plate, but I saw dogs, pulling and straining at their leashes. "Ain't very hungry this morning," I muttered and pushed back from the table.

Just before I left for school, Mama brought up the cat again. "You stick to the road," she cautioned as she poured heated water into her dishpan.

"Don't think you need to worry, Mama. Not so far from the city."

"Still, it's better to be safe," she said as I went out.

I stood on the porch for a minute, looking at the dew on the grass and listening to the rooster call out his good morning. I pulled myself up straight. I would not think about Lucky. Likely that big cat was far away, and besides, he was not my problem.

But there wasn't no forgetting the leopard. Buddy was waiting for me, and he was bent on discussing the search. "Wish I had me a gun," he said, "just in case that cat shows up." He held his finger up like a rifle and fired at a tree. "Pow."

I felt my throat getting tight again. "They don't want it shot," I told him. "I read about it in the newspaper last night."

Buddy laughed. "That thing comes on our place, I'm shooting it. Ain't taking no chances with our stock. Besides, a thing that big could kill a man."

"I'll bet he wouldn't," I protested. "Likely he'd be too scared to attack a person. Besides, he's used to the zookeeper and all."

Buddy shook his head. "Still, I'd like to bring it down. Maybe get the head fixed up for the wall real nice."

I tried not to react, just shrugged my shoulders. "Not likely to be around here." I decided to tell him about the Cadillac. "Boy, I saw the slickest car yesterday," I said, and I started telling the whole story with lots of little details.

Maybe I could have kept the conversation off Lucky if the Cansters hadn't showed up again.

"You want a ride, boys?" Mr. Canster said when he pulled up alongside us. He spit tobacco out the open window, and we jumped back to miss the dark stream.

"Thanks," I said, "but we'll just walk."

Instead of driving on like I had hoped, he leaned further out toward us. "Suit your ownself," he said. "Me, I ain't about to take no chance with my younguns. Reckon I'll be toting them to school till that cat's caught."

With a quick glance at the back of the truck, I took in the dirty faces of the little Cansters and wanted to protest that Lucky wasn't likely to get that hungry.

Mr. Canster went on talking. "Guess your daddies will be out looking for the beast. Bunch of us heading out about sundown, got lights and all." His teeth showed in a yellow grin. "Like to have me a leopard-skin rug."

"My father ain't home," I said. I turned away from the truck, and I pulled Buddy with me.

"Where you meeting?" Buddy said, but Mr. Canster didn't hear because he had given the truck gas and was moving on.

"You wouldn't go out hunting with him!" I twisted my face to show my disgust. "Fool likely shoot you by mistake."

"Well," Buddy started, but he was interrupted. School was just over the next little hill, and we could hear the bell.

"Dang bell," Buddy said, and we started to run.

While we were running an idea came to me, something to take our minds off the leopard and keep Buddy busy. We were lined up behind the little kids before I had a chance to tell him.

Mr. Whipple had taken over the bell, and he was giving it his all, pulling on the rope with a mighty force.

"I hate that bell," I whispered.

"Me too," Buddy agreed.

"We'll get the clapper," I said softly. "Come Monday, Mr. Whipple will pull on that rope, but won't nothing happen. Girls will go right on jumping rope, boys'll just keep playing marbles. Won't nobody run for school because that bell won't make a sound."

We laid our plans at noon while we had our dinner. Usually we ate under the same tree as the rest of the upper-grade kids, but this time we went off to ourselves and hunkered down in the shade by the side of the building.

"Can't anyone ever know about this," I told Buddy as I opened my lunch bucket. "No bragging or even hinting to them." I leaned my head in the direction of the others. "Mr. Whipple would most likely beat us to death, but it wouldn't matter anyhow. If there was any breath left in my body, my papa would finish the job."

Buddy was stuffing corn bread into his mouth, but he managed one word. "When?"

"Tonight. We'll have to wait until late, after everyone is asleep. Might be extra long at my house on account of Jessie coming home."

"Well, then," Buddy pulled my mind back to the bell, "what time you figure?"

I was working on a piece of smoke-cured pork Mama had stuck in my lunch bucket, and it required some serious chewing. Of course, Buddy wasn't likely to complain about my manners, but chomping on the meat gave me a chance to think. Finally I swallowed. "Tell you what. You go on to bed, go to sleep if you want, but leave your window up, the one by your bed. I'll reach in to give you a shake."

"Sounds like a winner. What then?"

"I'll bring a flashlight." I looked over at the bell. "It's one shinny up that pole and bye-bye, clapper."

All afternoon, me and Buddy grinned over our schoolwork. On the way home I kept Buddy talking about the bell joke. I just could not stand to hear him talk like Mr. Canster, about how killing a leopard would be great fun.

I set a pretty good walking pace, too. Lots had to be done before supper. First I would go over to Uncle Delbert's, see what was going on, and read the newspaper.

Then I would cut through the pasture again, and I'd look at everything real careful. I started thinking maybe they'd caught Lucky already. The idea struck me like a punch in my stomach. You're acting crazy, I told myself. Why in the dickens do you want to go and get all mixed up in some leopard's problems?

"This bell thing," I said to Buddy. "It's a great way to end the year."

I waited until we came to the cutoff by the bridge to say anything about heading to Uncle Delbert's. "Promised I'd work around there some." I lied because I sure didn't want company.

"Don't forget tonight," he said, and he laughed.

"Our greatest strike against the Whipper in his battle to make us upstanding citizens," I answered. It felt good just to be having fun with Buddy.

I yanked off his straw hat, tossed it into the air, and ran. "Don't scream like a fraidy cat when I shake you tonight," I yelled back over my shoulder. It was probably good that I was too far away to hear his answer.

Moving across the pasture, I kept my eyes wide open. Nothing seemed different. "You'd know if he was out there," I said to myself. "You'd feel him." Then I shook my head. Horsefeathers, I thought. You've gone completely loco. I concentrated on the Deluxe Tourist Court, trying to figure out what had been going on yesterday. When I got there, the Cadillac was still parked in front of cabin 3. Clientele staying over, that was real unusual. Uncle Delbert was in the restaurant, sweeping at the floor.

"Need to get this place in top condition," he told me. "Some very important people going to be eating here tonight."

"Who?" I asked as I climbed on a stool for my usual whirl.

Aunt Maybell came in right then, though, and Uncle Delbert rolled his eyes in her direction as a signal to drop the subject.

"How about apple for a change?" my aunt said, and she gave me the first piece of the big pie she carried. "Hope your supper won't be spoiled. I expect Maud's fixing something special with Jessie coming in and all."

The pie was still warm, with a golden crust, tender and sweet. I didn't want to do anything but eat, but Aunt Maybell settled herself on the stool beside me. "Maybe your papa will be with you for supper tonight," she said. "That job's bound to end soon."

I nodded, but kept shoveling in the pie.

Aunt Maybell made a sad sort of clucking with her tongue. "Money's hard to come by, but I won't be sorry to see that WPA work finished. Hobert's a man that yearns for family."

I worried about having Papa and Jessie both home at the same time. Jessie's college talk was sure to set him to storming around again.

"Be real nice seeing Jessie," Aunt Maybell went on. "You tell her we'll be looking for a visit."

"She'll be sure to come," I said around a mouthful.

Aunt Maybell didn't mention my manners, just patted my hand. "Reckon I'd better get back to the kitchen." She slid off the stool and lumbered toward the door.

As soon as she disappeared, Uncle Delbert stopped sweeping and came over to stand near me. "Ralph Summers," he said real soft. "He's a big oil man, awful big. Having dinner with one of his investors tonight." His voice swelled with pride. "Mighty important business getting conducted right here."

I was disappointed. The oil business didn't seem all that exciting. I watched Uncle Delbert go to each table to rearrange salt and pepper shakers. I wondered why he was so worked up.

The *Daily Oklahoman* was on the counter again, and Lucky looked up at me from the front page. It was a picture of him in his pit, crouched and miserable on the concrete. I didn't like the picture one bit. One of the stories said the experts were beginning to think maybe the leopard had traveled out of Oklahoma County into one of the surrounding counties. I took a deep breath. It was possible, then, possible for the cat to be in Lincoln County, maybe in my very own pasture. It was too much to take sitting still, so I whirled my stool real fast.

Uncle Delbert hovered by the window, but a little back. "Don't want to seem nosy," he said. "Rather they didn't see me watching."

I went over to look. Mr. Summers stood in front of his cabin. A tall, skinny man got into a nice blue Ford.

"Wonder where the fellow's going. They wasn't supposed to be here to eat this early." Uncle Delbert turned and scurried toward the kitchen. "Maybell," he called. "When will the chicken and dumplings be ready?"

"Be ready when it's ready," came from behind the door.

While I watched, the man in the car drove away. "He's gone," I told Uncle Delbert when he hurried back in.

He hesitated just a minute, leaning against the pop box. "Reckon it wouldn't be none out of the way to go out and inquire as to the supper plans." He moved pretty quick to the door, but I caught up to him.

Uncle Delbert was hotfooting it down the steps, but I could see there wasn't any rush. Mr. Summers had seen him and lingered in front of cabin 3.

"Couldn't help noticing that car driving away," my uncle said after the two men had exchanged greetings. He looked down at the grass. "My missus, she was sort of wondering as to whether you'd still be dining with company this evening."

Mr. Summers shook his head. "Poor fool. He's backing out." He took a big white handkerchief from his pocket and wiped at his face. "Hate to see him miss such a grand opportunity, him having a family and all."

"Some men just ain't got vision," said Uncle Delbert.

"Oh," answered Mr. Summers, "Jamison has got vision, all right. Just lets his wife control him, that's the problem. It's a pity, a pure pity." He shook his head, regret in his voice and face.

"I always say it's a thousand wonders how some men allow their womenfolk all the say-so." Uncle Delbert glanced toward the restaurant.

I looked too. Aunt Maybell stood in front of the window. I figured she would come out any minute, and I wanted to get another look at that Cadillac before she did. I inched toward it.

Behind me I heard Mr. Summers say, "The boy's real interested in my machine. You reckon your missus would object if we took him for a ride?"

"Why, there ain't no need to consult Maybell." Uncle Delbert hurried toward me. He was up with me in no time, and we climbed into the Cadillac without waiting for Mr. Summers.

In the back, I ran my hands over the fancy seat covers, but all the time I looked back. Aunt Maybell wasn't at the window anymore, but it seemed like it took Mr. Summers a long time to get behind the wheel.

I didn't really breathe right until the engine started and we pulled out. Looking back, I saw Aunt Maybell on the motel steps. She had her hands on her hips.

Out on the road, I forgot all about my aunt. Mr. Summers drove fast at first. I had the window down, listening to the swish of the tires on Highway 66 and letting the April breeze lift my hair. I felt like a million dollars.

When we came up behind a black Model-T, Mr. Summers called back to me. "Lean up here, son. Give the horn a good blast. People who drive old machines like that one got to learn how to get out of the way for a modern automobile."

Without looking at the driver of the older car, I reached up and pushed on the horn, not once but three times. The blast filled the car. With a mighty "Whoopie," I fell back into my seat and turned to wave at the Model-T.

There holding tight to the wheel was Mr. Whipple. He leaned forward, his lips pressed together. I slipped down in my seat, hoping he hadn't got a good look at me.

Still, I took great joy in the ride. Mr. Summers was a man among men. I studied the back of his big head and shoulders. Someday I would be just like him, with grand clothes, a diamond ring, and a shiny Cadillac.

"You want to drive her?" Mr. Summers asked my uncle.

"Thank you, but I don't believe I will. Not used to so much power."

"I imagine you'll be wanting to buy a new automobile, though." He looked over at my uncle. "Your place is doing real fine, isn't it?"

My heart started to pound, and I leaned up so as not to miss a word. I just couldn't give up the idea that Uncle Delbert might come through for Jessie.

"Well, now, I reckon we're doing all right, but a man has to be careful."

"You'll expand, though. Fellow like you is always looking ahead." Mr. Summers had slowed and now he turned back toward the tourist court. He didn't pick up speed, and I noticed he kept glancing at Uncle Delbert like he was really studying him.

"Sure, I'd like to expand, start with another place over in the next county." He shrugged his shoulders. "Don't know as I ever can, really. Takes capital, you know."

"See what you mean. I certainly do. Always say, 'Takes money to make money.' I told that to Jamison."

"Real shame about him," said Uncle Delbert.

"Sure is, and it's a shame you don't own your place free and clear. Then you could mortgage and invest in my leases. Make more than enough for another tourist court."

"Um," was all Uncle Delbert said.

I was leaning up, my arm resting on the back of the front seat, and I forgot I was not really included in the conversation. "He does," I blurted out. "He owns the entire Deluxe Tourist Court. Tell him, Uncle Delbert."

"You don't say?" said Mr. Summers.

"Well, yes, it's a fact. Sold my land to build the place. So far it takes just about what we make to keep us going."

"You could take out a loan against the business, though." He was still watching Uncle Delbert as much as he could and drive.

My uncle moved around some, like he wasn't so comfortable on the fine seat. "Don't know as we'd want to take a chance like that. Could lose our whole business."

"Just a thought," said Mr. Summers. "Just a thought."

I had a thought too about how the land that paid for the Deluxe Tourist Court had really belonged to Aunt Maybell, been in our family for years. I knew my aunt wouldn't be interested in taking any chance with mortgage loans, but I also knew it wasn't my place to say so.

We were back at the court's driveway. Mr. Summers stopped and turned to me. "You want to take her on in, son?" he asked me.

"Can I?" I was opening the rear door. "Can I really?"

"Why not?" said Uncle Delbert. "A man's got to get used to the finer things in life."

I climbed in fast and was ready to go. The steering wheel felt just right in my hand, but I guess the clutch wasn't like the one on the old truck. I must have let my foot off too quick because the gravel flew everywhere.

"Whew," yelled Mr. Summers, but he didn't tell me to stop.

I hated for the ride to end. The men got right out, but I stayed behind the wheel, pretending I was the owner. I started wondering how it would be to own a fancy car. Wouldn't me and Buddy have a time in a car like this? I'd even take Ring for rides. I'd give him a bath, brush him up real shiny, and let him ride up on the front seat beside me. We'd put the windows down, drive fast, and honk at every jackrabbit and cow.

For a while I didn't pay any mind to the conversation going on where Uncle Delbert and Mr. Summers were sprawled back in the cane-bottom chairs right outside the car window. Then I started to catch a real interesting word or two. I gave up daydreams and listened.

Mr. Summers took a big cigar out of a silver case and bit off the end, spitting into the grass. He offered the case to Uncle Delbert.

"Thank you." Uncle Delbert took a cigar and with a sidelong glance toward the restaurant stuck it in his pocket. "I'll just save this till later, after supper."

Mr. Summers nodded. "Nothing better, nothing better." He tilted his chair to balance on two legs and leaned his head back, releasing the sweet-smelling smoke in little puffs of white.

Uncle Delbert smiled and his words echoed Mr. Summers's. "Yes, sir, I always say nothing better than a good cigar after a meal."

I knew then Uncle Delbert was wanting real bad to agree with Mr. Summers because I had never in all my life seen my uncle smoke.

Mr. Summers nodded again and breathed deep. "Nothing better, that's for sure." Suddenly he snapped his chair upright and leaned forward, tapping Uncle Delbert's knee. "Nothing, that is, Del, except a speedy return on a man's money."

I stayed in the car, still sort of daydreaming about

driving and enjoying the smell of wax and leather mixed with the smoke of Mr. Summers's cigar. Every once in a while I'd catch bits of the men's conversation. Once Mr. Summers said, "Del, I just knowed you was a man of vision."

About that time Aunt Maybell came up on the other side from the men. She kind of leaned around the car to speak. "Them chicken and dumplings are ready, and the bread won't stay hot forever."

"I ain't sure our guest is ready to eat, Maybell," Uncle Delbert said, and he sounded embarrassed.

"Why, I swear, it'd take a puny man not to be ready for chicken and dumplings."

The men started toward the restaurant, but Aunt Maybell lingered. She bent down and stuck her head in the window. "Better head home, H.J.," she said. "Your mama will be wondering."

I got out, but I turned back and caressed the bright fender. "Ain't it just the grandest car, though?" I said to Aunt Maybell when I realized she was watching me.

"Well, yes." She wiped her hand across her eyes. "But, H.J., I don't want you to go building air castles. Your uncle, he can't help doing that sometimes, but I'd hate to see you take it up."

From where we stood it was easy to see Uncle Delbert holding the restaurant door for Mr. Summers. They were both laughing. I wanted to tell Aunt Maybell not to fret about Mr. Summers, that he was a real up-standing man, and that someday I'd be just like him. But I didn't say anything because I knew Mama would say such talk would show I was getting too big for my breeches.

Aunt Maybell's face was just full of uneasiness. I reached out and patted her shoulder. "I reckon I'd better go."

After just a ways, I looked back to wave, but my aunt didn't notice. She was walking real slow toward the restaurant, and she kept her eyes on the grass.

Thinking about everything that had just happened kept my mind off the leopard until I crawled between the fence wires and got onto our place. I was hightailing it along pretty good when something bolted from the trees and ran toward me. I jerked myself up, ready to tear out of there, until I realized it was Ring.

My hand was still shaking a little when I bent down to pet him. "What you doing out here?" Ring always waited for me at the house because I came home from school so many different ways.

The peculiar thing was that Ring didn't seem at all interested in being petted or in walking with me. Instead he shot toward the trees, barking. Even when I whistled, he didn't turn back.

Naturally, my mind went straight to that leopard. Was he stretched in the sand under that cottonwood again? For a minute I considered heading for home, real fast, but of course I couldn't leave Ring. Besides, if Lucky was out there, I had to see him, had to look into those strange yellow eyes one more time. Just the thought of it sent a shiver up my backbone.

Ring didn't come back, but suddenly he stopped barking. Everything seemed extra quiet. Not even a crow was cawing. My feet got real heavy, but I forced them to move across the grass toward the woods.

Just before I reached the first tree, Ring appeared again. "What is it, boy?" I called, and my words seemed to bounce off the silence around me.

Ring stayed where he was, his hair all ruffled up on the back of his neck. I'd seen him hunt before, but that was different. Usually when he chased a rabbit or got something treed, his tail would go a mile a minute, just wagging all over the place.

This time, though, his tail was sort of tucked down. I knew then that Ring was dead serious about whatever was in those trees. He growled way back in his throat. It was the deepest, most fierce growl I had ever heard him make.

"We better skedaddle," I said, but I didn't move. Instead I stared across the grass and into the branches of the woods. Ring was in front of me. When I finally decided to walk, I had to force him out of my way.

"Just a little ways, boy. Just far enough to get a look."

I took another step, pushing Ring with my leg. He was doing his best to block my steps.

Most of the trees were green. Suddenly I realized the one I stood beneath was big and full. Maybe the leopard was up there watching me. Very slowly, I put back my head. The leopard's spots would sort of mix with the shadows among the leaves, and he would be really hard to see. Holding my breath, I rolled my head from side to side, searching the branches. Ring didn't budge, just stayed pressed against me. Every once in a while he would whimper real soft, and I knew he was begging me to leave. I couldn't though. My mind was full of how I told Buddy that the leopard wasn't likely to jump a man because he was used to zoo people. Had I told the truth? Maybe Ring and I were about to find out.

I put out my foot to ease a little further into the trees, but I didn't forget to look up before I walked under one. The thing was, I failed to look down. Suddenly my foot gave way as I stepped into a hole, and I felt myself falling.

The ground that met me was hard, hard enough to knock the wind out of me, and it took a minute for me to realize what had happened. Ring stood over me. The scary thing was that he didn't lick at me, didn't even look down at me. The hair on his neck still stuck up, and his growl was even more ferocious than before.

Every inch of me was shaking. Sure, I wanted to see

Lucky, but I hadn't planned to be stretched out on my back like a turned-over turtle when we met.

After a minute, I forced my head up just a little. That's when I saw it. There off to my side was an animal, or what was left of it. I raised myself a little more, and I could see it was a deer, a dead deer.

My gaze darted all around. No leopard in sight, so I had the nerve to scramble back up on my feet with the help of a possum grapevine to pull on. "He's not here," I told Ring. "See, there ain't nothing to be scared of."

He stopped growling, and my courage started to grow. I brushed off my overalls, and found the nerve to walk right over to the deer. It was a buck, big and powerful. His throat was bloody. So were his hindquarters, and there were great long marks, cat scratches.

I leaned down for one quick touch to prove what I knew must be true, and it was. The skin felt warm. Suddenly my skin wasn't warm at all.

Just a few minutes earlier this buck had been alive, and it had been attacked by a cat. Something had been in this very spot, something big enough to bring down a large deer. I had never heard of a bobcat killing a buck.

He was out there, not far away. I knew he was, and I was standing over his dinner. Even a leopard used to people was bound to be riled by that.

"Let's go," I whispered to Ring. Boy, did I want to make a run for home, but I took a deep breath instead.

"Slow," I said. "Nice and slow." If Lucky watched from some secret spot, I was pretty sure he would be more likely to go for me if I was running.

Back out in open pasture, I felt better, but my heart still pounded. "It could have been sick or injured somehow," I told Ring. "A bobcat could kill a buck if it was already down."

I stepped along through the new grass and clover, and I tried to sell myself the bobcat story. It was hard for me to face the sure and certain truth about Lucky the leopard. I knew, though. I knew he waited somewhere out in the trees on my very own homeplace. I would see that big cat again, and it would be an important meeting. The sun was getting low. I stopped and looked back at the trees, and a kind of shiver went over me. I would find Lucky, or he would find me.

5

THE DICKERSONS' OLD CHEVY pulled away from our house just as I got there. Howard was driving, and I figured he had taken his father home before dropping Jessie off at our house. He honked the horn real long and waved at me. I sort of felt sorry for Howard. Him and Jessie had been sweet on each other off and on for years, but I knew Jessie was ready to leave him behind without looking back if she could go to college.

Mama and Jessie were in the kitchen unpacking the groceries Jessie had brought home from Henson's store. For a few minutes I stood on the porch listening to their voices drift through the window. I couldn't go busting in there, not till I had time to stand for a minute. Mama always could look at me and see when I was up to something.

I ran my palms across my face to wipe the sweat off, took a deep breath, and tried to get myself back to normal. I could smell fried potatoes and pinto beans. Hunger pulled at me to go on into the house.

I decided to go on in and think only about Jessie being

home or about the bell joke, not the leopard. Ring was still beside me. I bent and gave him a fast hug, then went through the front door and let it bang behind me.

"I was about to figure you'd have a cold supper," Mama called out.

I hesitated just a second in the front room to practice a regular smile. It was Jessie who noticed how I looked. "You've been running," she said when she came over to sort of brush my hair back from my face, which was most usually the way she told me hello. She glanced toward the window and grinned. "Is Mr. Whipple chasing you with his paddle?"

I forced a little laugh. "Think I lost him in the south pasture."

"What's this?" Mama held up a brown paper sack with words printed in pencil on the side.

Real quick Jessie was beside Mama and reaching. "My beans," she said. "That silly Howard weighed them up for me."

Mama stuck out her elbow so Jessie couldn't take the sack. "Roses are red, violets are blue, don't go off to college and make me miss you," she read.

"It's a joke," said Jessie. "I didn't know he wrote on it." Her face started turning red.

"There's more." Mama stepped away with the sack and turned it around. "Roses are red, violets are blue, orange hair sure does look pretty on you."

"He's just teasing me." Jessie shook her head.

"Ain't much of a poet," I said.

"But a real devoted one." Mama gave Jessie the sack and a little hug. "I didn't order beans, did I?"

"I wanted to make sure we had plenty. Need a bunch to count." Jessie walked over to the cabinet and took down a big gallon jar. "There's a contest just for our senior class," she said. "There's a jar like this in the bank window. Whoever guesses how many beans are in it gets fifty dollars."

"I bet old Howard'd like to come over and help you count." I was at the washstand with my hands all soaped up. Jessie picked up my towel and popped me with it.

"You can help me," she said.

"Speaking of beans." Mama handed Jessie the green onions and took the lid off the bean pot. "We're ready to eat."

Nobody talked while we filled our plates, and I started thinking about how Jessie wanted that fifty dollars to go in her college fund. "Shoot, Jessie," I said when we settled at the table, "Uncle Delbert might change his mind and give you money for college. I bet he will if he makes a bunch on a good deal."

It was the wrong thing to say, and I knew it even before the words were completely out.

I could feel Mama's eyes on me and Jessie's too. "Papa doesn't want me taking money from Uncle

Delbert," Jessie said, but there was a hopeful look on her face. I figured if Jessie got offered the money, she'd find a way to take it.

"What's going on at Delbert's?" Mama demanded.

I had stuffed my mouth and motioned toward it with my fork. Didn't Mama preach against talking and chewing? So I had a second to think.

Mama didn't wait long. "Out with it," she said.

"Well, I just meant that Uncle Delbert's likely to be pretty big in the tourist court business, that's all. He's got vision." I filled my spoon with more beans.

"That fellow in the fancy vehicle still at the court?"

"Uh-huh, I guess so." This didn't seem to be the time to tell about the ride and about how I had been allowed to drive the car into the driveway.

Mama wasn't finished. "And Maybell don't like this man. Is that right?"

I shrugged my shoulders. "He's a paying customer. I reckon she likes that."

"Maybe we'll just drive over there tomorrow if we can get the truck started."

"Let's walk," said Jessie. "Have a nice springtime hike."

"No." I was reaching for my glass and almost knocked it over. "Not through the pasture." They were looking at me again, expecting more. "They say that leopard likely ain't in Oklahoma County anymore, that's all."

Jessie pushed back her chair. "We can eat our cobbler in the front room. Maybe there's news on the radio. I'm real interested in that leopard, aren't you, H.J.?"

"Guess so." I followed Jessie into the other room. I went over and leaned against the top of the big old radio while Jessie fooled with the dial. She was frowning, trying to find a station. "We could sure use a new radio," I said.

"What did you mean about Uncle Delbert?" she asked.

I knew it wasn't right, me getting her hopes up when I didn't really know nothing about what was going on. I sort of shrugged. "I think it's possible he'll help you yet," I said. "Seems like it don't hurt to hope."

I couldn't look at my sister, though, because I knew she was hurting, hurting real bad. I was glad when she got the radio going, but there wasn't any news about Lucky. "Poor thing," said Jessie while she changed stations. "I feel sorry for it, being hunted like that. Hope no one gets carried away and shoots it."

I couldn't get my mind on the program even when the Shadow was about to get the bad guys. I got up and walked out to the porch. I wanted to think about the bell clapper, but in my imagination I kept seeing Lucky, his eyes shining out in the night.

I thought Mama and Jessie never would go to bed. When I went back in the house, they were caught up in listening to news on the radio. Mama worried over that fellow named Hitler over in Germany. Seems he was taking boys as young as ten and teaching them to be soldiers.

The radio man said Hitler had threatened a nearby country named Poland. The leader of England was promising his country would take up for Poland if Germany tried anything.

I flopped beside Mama on the divan. She reached over and touched my cheek. "Sure am glad my boy ain't over there in Germany," she said.

Jessie rocked in the old wooden chair. "My history teacher thinks if war breaks out in Europe, we won't be able to stay out of it." She glanced at me. "It could last a long time."

Mama had popped us popcorn, and I tossed a piece at Jessie. "Ooops," I said. It worked and Jessie forgot all the serious stuff. Mama didn't even tell us to stop, but the talk about buying headache powders was over. The man was going on about Hitler again.

Mama and Jessie were both leaning toward the radio, real interested. I just wanted to get on with the bell thing, so I yawned, hoping they would sort of catch the feeling.

"Why don't you go on to bed, son?" Mama said to me, but she didn't look sleepy.

I went into my room. Pretty soon Mama and Jessie turned off the radio, but in the kitchen they spread patterns out on the table and talked about a new dress Jessie was making from the flowered material Aunt Maybell gave her for Christmas.

I stretched out on my bed, listening until finally they said good night and put out the lights. Still, I had to wait. My shoes were on the floor, but I had left on my clothes. I knew Mama might look into my room, so I pulled the sheet up over my overalls.

The flashlight was next to me. I sure hoped the batteries would hold up. The moon seemed good and bright. Maybe I wouldn't need the light until time to work on the bell.

While I waited, I listened. My window was open, and the tree frogs filled the air with their music. Out in the lot Bossy bawled out real quick. I wondered if something might have scared her, but after that once she was quiet.

When I was sure Mama and Jessie had to be asleep, I reached for my shoes and the flashlight. Real careful, I eased the window up. No one stirred inside the house.

The screen was held by only one hinge. It would come off if I pushed. Mama and Jessie, on the other side of the house, wouldn't hear it fall.

Ring did, though. He was there waiting and barking

when I hit the ground. "Ssh," I said. "We don't want to wake anyone up. We're just going to have us a nice walk in the moonlight."

Bossy bawled again, and she sounded excited. "Maybe we'd better check the cow lot before we take off."

At the corner of the house, I sort of held my breath, but nothing was in sight. Bossy was near the gate, and she had her head up. I walked over to the fence and scratched her neck. "Go to sleep, you silly old cow," I said. "You just don't like being shut up."

She shook her head and snorted like she wanted to protest. I patted her one more time. Then me and Ring headed toward the road.

It seemed darker out there away from the house. Buddy's place was a mile away. I steadied myself for a lonely walk. Ring, though, enjoyed every step, just loped along beside me, not watchful or barking.

"There's nothing out there, is there, boy? You'd know, wouldn't you?" I felt better, but my fists were still clenched.

Talking out loud gave me courage, so I decided to recite. "How much wood would a woodchuck chuck, if a woodchuck could chuck wood?" I was on a roll. "Hey, Ring," I said, "want to know how to spell Chicago? CHicken In the Car, And the Car won't Go. That's how you spell Chicago." Next came Mississippi,"M, i, crooked letter, crooked letter, i, crooked letter, crooked letter, i, double p . . ." I was about to say the last *i* when a noise from a nearby tree made me swallow my words.

I grabbed Ring, then froze. I yelled out, though, when suddenly a great black hawk flew out of the tree and over my head. "A bird won't hurt us," I said, but my heart didn't stop pounding.

Something had disturbed the bird's sleep. I turned to look back the way I had come. If I lit out, I could be home in my bed in a flash. Buddy was likely asleep anyway. We could get the bell some other time or think of another way to get a laugh on Mr. Whipple. No one would ever have to know about me running home, afraid.

My legs started to move. I would know, though. I would know I was scared to walk down a road in the bright moonlight. I shook my head. "No sirree," I said real loud. "H.J. Harper ain't no fraidy cat."

I forced my foot to take a step forward. "We got to quit this fooling around and make tracks," I told Ring. He seemed to understand what I meant, and he bounded ahead. I had to trot to stay up with him.

It was better that way. Moving fast didn't give me a chance to hear every little rustle of leaves in the trees beside the road.

By the time we got to Buddy's, I was feeling pretty

brave. "Stay here and wait," I told Ring when we were in front of the house. I didn't want Buddy's dogs, Mutt and Jeff, to start barking and carrying on.

"It's me, just H.J.," I said when the dogs came running at me. Mutt was a great big dog, but it was little Jeff that took a hunk out of the leg of a man who had come by the week before wanting to sell a magazine subscription or trade one for any old car batteries the McDanielses had around.

Mutt calmed down right off, but Jeff kept jumping up on me. He didn't make much racket, though. The whole house stayed dark. I figured it must be 10:30 by now. No one would be up at such an hour.

Buddy had the screen off his window, ready. He had his clothes off. I could see him there on his back in his red long johns.

I had to stretch up to my tiptoes to reach his shoulder, but I gave it a good shake. "Wake up," I whispered, but he rolled over on his stomach.

Now I could only reach his arm, and I pinched it good.

"Heck." He jerked himself into a upright position.

"It's me, H.J." I pulled myself up by the sill and stuck my head into the window. "Remember?"

He leaned close, staring at my face. "I never noticed till this minute," he said, "but I got to say you're dog ugly."

"And I reckon you're a dandy sight in your red winter johns." I slapped at the air in his direction.

"I get cold." He yawned, and I was afraid he was about to stretch out again.

"You coming out or do I crawl in there and drag you?"

"OK. OK. Don't bust a gut." He scooted so he could put his legs over the side of the bed.

I dropped back to the grass and waited for what seemed like a long time for just pulling on overalls and shoes, but finally he climbed out. "All right," I said. "Let's get going."

Buddy didn't move. Instead he turned his head slowly, looking all around him. "I don't know. That leopard could be out there. I heard a fellow on the radio say they didn't think it was up by the city anymore."

"You backing out?"

"Just thinking. If we go, I ought to take Daddy's gun."

"Your father wouldn't like that. We're taking chance enough sneaking out. You scared?"

My argument worked, and we started moving.

The McDaniels place was all lit up by the moon. I could see the chicken house and the big tree where Mutt and Jeff had settled back down for the night, but I could only see to the fence. Lucky, I pleaded silently, if you're out there, don't show yourself.

I knew Buddy wouldn't keep Lucky secret, and I made sure to stay in the middle of the road so Buddy would too, and most of the time I held to the hair on the back of Ring's neck. If Lucky was out there, he would stay off to the side in the dark trees.

It seemed like a good idea too to get Buddy's mind off leopards. I started talking about what would happen when Mr. Whipple tried to ring the bell on Monday. "Reckon he'll cuss?" I asked. "Boy, I sure do hope he cusses."

"His face is bound to get red. Probably redder than we ever seen it." Buddy grinned big, and I saw that he paid no attention to the woods beside us.

"You think he'll climb up to see what's wrong?"

Buddy laughed. "Naw, more likely he'll send someone up. Hope it's you or me."

"What we going to say?" I asked.

"My goodness, sir. The clapper's missing. Now ain't that just the strangest thing?" Buddy quit walking and bent over laughing.

"And none of that," I warned. "We let out one little chuckle, and we're dead. Right now, though, we need a plan for getting this thing done. Just one of us can go up."

"You," said Buddy. "It was your idea."

"You can just forget that part if we get caught." I laughed. "Don't you be saying, 'It was H.J.'s idea.'"

"Hey, now, you know I ain't no squealer." He slapped at my arm.

Before long we could see the school with its new coat of red paint. There in front was the pole with the huge bell, the bell we were about to conquer. I let out a whoop and started to run.

The bell pole and the flagpole were just alike, both tall and made of steel. They were held solid in cement. We leaned against them and looked up.

"Hey, I got an idea," said Buddy. "After we fix the bell, how about if I take off my long johns and we run them up the flagpole."

I hooted. "Great idea. Positively prime!" Then a thought came to me, and I shook my head. "Wait a minute. Mr. Whipple takes down the johns. He looks at the size, and he knows they belong to you, me, or that new kid in seventh grade. He figures they're yours or mine. He takes them by your house, and of course your mama says your red ones are missing."

"Yeah, yeah. I get it. But it would have made a fine sight, a bright red flag."

I stared up at the pole. "I'll need to take off my shoes and socks, get me a better hold."

"I'll give you a leg up," said Buddy, and he locked his hands into a stirrup.

It wasn't easy climbing that pole. I inched my way up, my hands and feet burning from their tight grip on the steel. Buddy called up encouraging words. "Good job. You're almost there."

A board fastened to the top of the pole where the bell rack was bolted in seemed made for my flashlight. Holding on with one hand, I took the light from my overalls pocket, turned it on, and set it on the board. "I can see real plain," I reported to Buddy. "The clapper just slides over a hook."

"Get her," he called. "Just warn me before you let her fall."

I had to work with one hand, but finally I had the big steel clapper loose and in my palm. "Stand back," I yelled, and I let the heavy piece slip through my fingers.

Buddy ran over to retrieve the clapper when it crashed against the cement. "Got it!" he shouted. "Come on down."

"On my way," I answered, but I wasn't. When I picked up the flashlight, I didn't turn it off and put it in my pocket. Something made me shine it around the school yard instead.

Over to my left by the fence, two points of light glittered in the reflected beam of the light. I sucked in my breath sharp.

"You caught on something?" Buddy's voice floated up to me, sounding like he was a great distance away.

"No," I managed to mutter softly. "I'm coming." I

moved the flashlight a little and right there caught in the shaft of light was the great beast's head and its long body.

I froze, afraid Ring would smell Lucky and take to growling, but the wind lifted my hair. I breathed a little. We were upwind from the cat. I held tight to the pole.

"What is it?" Buddy called. "Why don't you come on down?" Lucky was looking into my light. I don't know how long I might have hung there, spellbound, if the cat hadn't moved first. With a mighty whirl, he turned and ran, headed for the trees north of the school.

"H.J., is something wrong up there?"

"No." It was the only word I could get out. I slid down the pole.

6

IT WAS HARD WORK acting normal with Buddy. We stopped by the bridge and dug out a hole in the ground with a stick. "Rest in peace," Buddy said as I dropped in the clapper, "and we too shall have peace." Then he looked around a minute and found a good-sized rock to put on top.

All the way to his house I tried to laugh and plan about how it would be at school come Monday. A couple of times he had to poke me and repeat what he had said. "Getting real tired," I explained. It was sure enough true. My head whirled and my body ached with the weight of knowing for sure that a leopard moved along the same trails I followed every day.

Back at home, there wasn't any sense in trying to sleep. I settled myself on the front porch steps. Ring stretched out on the ground near my feet.

The voice of the tree frogs mixed with the call of a whippoorwill, but the familiar sounds seemed different, somehow. Everything was changed because of that cat.

"Maybe it ain't right, me not telling anyone," I said to Ring. He held his head up to look at me. "I sure wish you could talk, boy," I said. "What if that cat gets old Bossy or one of our neighbor's cows. Can't none of us afford to lose stock."

I stood up. "Or what if it jumps a person. Mama maybe, or Jessie, or some little kid? I ought to go in there and wake Mama up. We could take the truck, drive over to Uncle Delbert's, and call the sheriff." I looked at the front door. "Maybe I ought to do it now," I said, but I sat back down on the step.

A coyote howled from over in the south pasture. Maybe it would find the dead buck. I hoped not, because if that leopard went back and finished the buck, he would be full for a while and not be going after other things.

I huddled on the porch for a long time. My eyes were getting heavy, but just when I thought I'd have to go to bed, ideas started coming to me. We'd go over to Aunt Maybell's tomorrow, like Mama said. I'd do more than just see what was happening with Uncle Delbert and Mr. Summers. I'd also talk to Aunt Maybell.

I'd tell her there were a couple of hungry dogs hanging around in the woods and ask her to save the restaurant scraps for me to feed them.

But before I did any of that, I'd get up early and go over to the south pasture and look around where that buck was. I wanted to see that cat in the daylight, wanted it real bad.

I was afraid using the front door might rouse Mama, so I stood up and started around the house to my window. "OK, boy," I said to Ring. "You get some sleep. I'll see you in the morning."

Sleep came just as soon as I was in bed. So did dreams. All the time I slept I dreamed about Lucky. He was huge, as big as a house, and he was running, running, running. His coat shined in the moonlight. The really crazy thing was that Aunt Maybell, Uncle Delbert, and Mr. Summers were running after him. I was behind them. I kept calling out for them to wait, but they just kept running.

I didn't wake up as soon as I wanted to. Mama was already in the kitchen. "You're up early," she said when I went sort of stumbling in.

"Thought I'd get the milking done and maybe go fishing for a while. A mess of fish would be pretty good."

Mama looked up from the bread she was kneading. "Reckon you ought to wake Jessie up? She might want to go."

I reached for the milk bucket. "Suspect she'd rather sleep late."

Mama nodded. "She looks a little peaked, probably don't get enough sleep."

If my sister didn't get enough sleep, I knew how she must feel. I was so weary that I almost fell down the porch steps. By the time I'd finished the milking, though, I was wide awake and ready for the biggest adventure of my life.

From the barn I took my pole and fishing stuff because Mama could be watching. I'd put it down once I was away from the house. Mama wouldn't be surprised when I came home empty-handed. Lots of times I didn't have much luck.

I also took a piece of rope. "I might have to put this around your neck," I told Ring. "Just in case you get too excited if we see the cat."

It was a great morning. Clover was starting to get thick in the field. Any other day I'd have shed my shoes just to feel the thick greenness on my bare feet. Even in my rush I looked down every once in a while. It couldn't hurt, I figured, if I found a four-leaf clover for luck.

At the edge of the woods, I stashed the fishing gear under the first tree. We hadn't walked ten feet till Ring started the growling. "Whoa, boy," I said, "it'll be all right." My arms were covered with goose bumps. I made a slipknot in the rope and put it around Ring's neck. He fussed some, but I smoothed the thick hair around the rope and talked him into calming down.

"Don't want you charging some big cat," I told him. "He might just slap the dickens out of you."

For a long time I didn't say anything else, not out loud anyway. I held Ring real close to me, and I kept talking to myself in my head. Every time a twig snapped under my foot, I'd think how all this would turn out good and how the leopard wasn't dangerous on account of being used to zoo workers.

We weren't far from where I had seen the deer when a big jackrabbit ran out of a log up ahead of me. Ring let out a howl and strained against the rope. "Hold it, boy," I whispered. "Be still now." He settled down, and I took time to pet him before we walked on.

When we were really close to the spot, I stopped. Ring was growling low, and I was sure we were near the leopard. I was sure too that the cat knew we were coming. "Hush," I told Ring real stern like. He did. Ring always did what I told him, the best dog in the world. I knew he wanted to growl, though. I could feel his body all stiff against my leg.

I saw the deer carcass first. Up in a big elm, it hung in the fork where the branches grew off from the trunk. Then I saw the leopard. He rested on a limb above the deer, and he was the most beautiful thing I had ever seen.

Ring growled. I whispered, "Hush." He pushed against my leg, wanting to get between me and the cat. It didn't look ready to jump, but I knew it could spring at us in a flash. Every muscle in my body was tense, but for some reason I wasn't terrified.

"Lucky," I said real soft. "Lucky, we won't hurt you. We want to be your friend."

For a long time, that leopard and me just looked at each other. His eyes were the color of the leaves and of the sun all mixed together, and I looked right into them. Not a sound disturbed us. Ring squirmed against me, but he didn't growl. Even the birds perched, silent, in the trees around us.

Finally, the big cat moved. His great muscles contracted and in a flash he landed on the other side of the tree from me. Ring bristled and let out his growl.

Lucky's front legs met his back legs smooth as water in the creek and he floated through the grass. "I'll protect you," I called after him. "I swear I will."

I leaned against the tree trunk in a kind of trance, staring at the limb where the leopard had crouched. My legs threatened to give way and pitch me headlong into the grass, and I pushed myself harder against the tree, my mind racing. I had seen Lucky. We had looked at each other and a sort of message passed between us. Then I had made that promise, that promise to protect him. After a while the rough tree bark started to dig into my skin because I didn't have a shirt under my overalls. I had to move, and I sort of came awake.

Ring knew something was going on. When I moved away from the tree, he trotted quietly beside me, and I felt the warm, reassuring lick of his tongue on my fingers.

I forgot my fishing pole and tackle box but remembered when I almost bumped into the tree where I'd left them. I picked up my gear and looked at it. It seemed like ages since I had dropped it there.

Out in the bright open pasture, I started to face what had happened back in the trees. I had promised to help Lucky, me against a bunch of experts, dozens of determined, grown-up men.

"You've got to be my only partner," I told Ring when I bent down to take the rope from his neck, "and it's a heck of a job." His whine sounded like a promise to help.

All the way home, I tried to come up with some way to keep Lucky from going back to the zoo. "He's got to have room, belongs in the mountains somewhere, but there ain't no way I could get him there," I explained to Ring, and when we crawled over the fence separating the pasture from our yard, I still didn't have any particle of an answer.

Mama and Jessie were feeding the chickens. "No luck, huh?" Mama called when she saw me. For a second I didn't know what she meant, but then I remembered the fishing pole.

"Not a bit of luck," I yelled. I sure hoped it wasn't true. I'd need lots of luck, and I'd need it soon.

Breakfast was over, but the biscuits and gravy waiting covered on the stove still felt warm. Jessie's beans and jar were still on the table where she'd been counting, but I wasn't interested right now.

I was sure hungry, but all the time I ate I pictured that cat, how it looked at me like it wanted to know me the next time we met. I imagined it running, and I quit chewing on the biscuit and bit at my lip. It sure seemed to me any animal that looked so beautiful loping across the grass ought to be free.

When the food was gone, I didn't move, just stared at my empty plate, seeing Lucky. That's how Mama found me. "You look kind of tuckered," she said, and she squeezed my shoulder. "Jessie and me are fixing to go over to see Maybell and Delbert. You up to going with us?"

I jumped up. "I'll fire up the truck."

Right quick, I got me a shirt on and went out to the truck. After about the third try, I had the old engine turning, and I honked the horn. Mama and Jessie came out and crowded into the seat beside me. With one backfire we were off. In the rearview mirror I saw Ring staring after us. I wished I had given him a good talking to about not leaving the yard.

Things had been sort of dry, and with every bounce of the truck, clouds of red dust flew into the windows. Mama and Jessie held handkerchiefs in front of their faces until we turned onto the highway, but the dust didn't bother me. Keeping control of that old truck as it lunged and lurched down the road took most of my attention. Still, my eyes were able to skim the fences and trees along the road for some sign of Lucky.

That cat didn't leave my mind for a second until we got to the Deluxe Tourist Court. Catching sight of the sign always thrilled me.

I was thinking about how Uncle Delbert might open another place when I noticed Mr. Summers and Uncle Delbert in the chairs under a big shade tree near cabin 3. I waved real big, but I guess they were too busy talking to notice.

"Is that the fellow you told us about?" Mama leaned around me to peer at Mr. Summers.

"That's him. Take a look at that Cadillac." Even before I killed the engine, I had the door open, ready to jump out and join the men.

Mama put her hand on my arm. "You come on inside with me and Jessie," she said. "Stay out of what don't concern you."

Aunt Maybell was in the kitchen cooking up the noon meal for the restaurant. Her face was red, and she swung hard at the carrots she chopped with her butcher knife.

Hugging Jessie and making over her took up some time, but Aunt Maybell got to Mr. Summers pretty soon. "Gab, gab," she complained as Mama and Jessie pulled up chairs to join her at the little table. "That's all Delbert's done since that fellow come. Just building air castles in the clouds."

"Is the man wanting to sell cars?" Mama asked.

"No. It's oil business he's in. If he's trying to sell Delbert anything, I ain't been told about it. They do a lot of big-shot jawing about investments and taking money to make money, though." She went back to her chopping. "Makes me uneasy. Supposed to leave tomorrow. That's one cabin I'll be glad to see empty."

Aunt Maybell made me feel sort of guilty about liking Mr. Summers, and I wanted to change the subject. "Howard Dickerson's been writing poems to Jessie," I said, and I climbed up on a chair. "Roses are red, violets are blue, ain't never seen a girl pretty as you." I spread my arms wide and made a fancy bow at the end.

"That's wrong." Jessie made a face at me. "Besides, Howard wouldn't say 'ain't.'"

Aunt Maybell dropped the knife and leaned toward Jessie. "Howard wanting to court you, is he?"

Jessie shrugged. "He's awful nice, that's all."

"Jessie's real anxious to make up the spring dress goods you gave her," Mama said.

"Well, if you must know, we're going to a picture show next Saturday night." Jessie tried to sound mad, but I could see she was anxious to tell. "It's *Robin Hood*, and Errol Flynn's the star."

"My, my." Aunt Maybell winked at Mama, then turned back to Jessie. "How you making the goods up, honey?"

Not being interested in dresses, I hopped down from

the chair and wandered out the back door. I was sitting on the back steps trying to figure how I'd find a chance to ask my aunt about the scraps when she came out.

"H.J.," she said. "A man named Hudson just called up on the telephone. Wanted me to tell that Summers fellow to wait for him. Says to say he's got the money now and is ready to sign." She wiped her hands on her apron. "I'd just as soon not go over there."

I jumped up. "Mr. Hudson," I repeated. "Says to wait for him. He's got the money now and is ready to sign."

"That's right." She turned to go back in.

"Aunt Maybell," I said. "I wanted to ask you about scraps."

"Scraps?"

"Yeah." I moved closer to her. "I don't want Mama to know 'cause she gets all nervous about strays." It wasn't easy for me to lie, and I had to look down. "See, there's these two big dogs hanging out in our south pasture. Just skin and bones. Don't figure they'll hold on much longer without food."

"So you're wanting my scraps?"

I nodded.

"Well, usually I let Bill Covey have 'em for his hogs." She hesitated. "Nice dogs, are they?"

"Real nice and awful hungry." I jammed my hands into my overall pockets and waited.

"Hate to see any animal starving." She nodded. "Reckon Bill Covey will just have to buy his hogs feed for a spell." She looked back at the door. "There's a nearly full bucket by the sink. You watch your chance to put it in the truck. Just be our little secret."

I gave her a quick hug. "Run on now," she said. "You remember the message?"

I told her I did. Then I dashed around the building toward the two men. "Mr. Summers," I yelled. "You got a phone call."

The big man shot out of his chair. "My wife?" he asked. "Is something wrong?"

"No." I was beside him by then, and I saw the relief on his face. "It was Mr. Hudson. Said to tell you he would be over soon. Said he had the money now and was ready to sign."

It was Uncle Delbert's face I noticed then. He sort of went white, and he looked like he'd just been slapped. Real interested, I waited till Mr. Summers settled back down in his chair. Then I found a spot on the grass where I could hear their conversation. I half expected Uncle Delbert to shoo me off, but he didn't.

My uncle took a white handkerchief out of his pocket. I figured this must be big stuff to make him sweat just resting there under a shade tree when it wasn't even hot summer yet. He wiped at his face as he talked. "What does this mean, Ralph? If you cut Hudson back in, what does that mean for me?"

"Well." Mr. Summers stood up, took a couple of steps, and came back.

Uncle Delbert leaned forward. "Well, what, Ralph? I'm waiting."

Mr. Summers drew in a big breath. He shook his head like he was in a lot of doubt. Then he lowered his heavy body back into the chair. "Damn it, Del," he said. "This leaves me between a rock and a hard place."

A bee swarmed around Uncle Delbert's face, but he didn't pay it any heed. "You promised me a chance. Said I could have time to talk to Maybell, make her see what an opportunity this could be for us."

Mr. Summers spread his big hands and looked at them. "Don't you see, Delbert. On one hand I've got Hudson. His place is not more than forty miles from here. He's on his way over here with money, and he's ready to sign. On the other hand there's you with a wife that's likely to object."

"Hudson's wife objected, didn't she?" Uncle Delbert got up to stand beside Mr. Summers.

"She did. Yes, she did that." He was speaking slowly, like he was trying to sort things out. "I like you, Del. My gut is sort of telling me to give you a chance."

"Do it." There was joy in Uncle Delbert's voice. "Give me till tomorrow. Just that long."

"I suppose I could stall him." He turned to put his hand on Delbert's shoulder. "Just till tomorrow, though, my friend. I can't wait any longer. This is business."

Uncle Delbert got up and walked over to the Cadillac with Mr. Summers, talking all the way. After Mr. Summers got in, Uncle Delbert leaned down into the car and kept right on talking.

I stayed in my spot, chewing on a grass blade and hoping my uncle would come back and explain it all to me. Even after Mr. Summers started the motor, Uncle Delbert hung on the car, talking. When the Cadillac started to move, I half expected to see him climb on the running board.

Mr. Summers honked the horn real loud and waved at me. I jumped to my feet and waved back. Uncle Delbert practically danced his way back to the shade tree. "I convinced him." He slapped at my shoulder and let himself fall into a chair. "This is big, H.J. This is real big."

He went on to explain about oil leases and about how Mr. Summers was fixing to buy up a bunch cheap because he had just happened to get the scoop on a fellow coming up from Texas to buy leases. Mr. Summers would sell what he had just bought to the Texas fellow. He'd make thousands and not even have to wait for the drilling.

"We can be in on this, H.J.," he said, putting his

head back on the chair and closing his eyes. "In a matter of weeks you and me could make enough money to build two more courts. We'll be in high cotton, boy."

Hearing him include me in the deal sent a shiver up my back, and a beginning of an idea to my head. "How you plan to get the money?" I asked.

"There's where the rub comes in." His voice took on a doubtful sound, and he rested his face in his hands. "It means taking out a mortgage, you know, a loan against this place." He shook his head. "Maybell won't like the risk. I told you before, your aunt ain't got vision."

"She's got to sign something?" I asked. "You can't just surprise her?"

"Boy," he said. "You just said right out what was going through my mind." He looked at me real straight. "The bank would take just my signature." He shook his head. "Don't know as that would be right. This place is all we got, and the land we sold to build it came from her pa, you know."

"Uncle Delbert," I said. "If you make a bunch of money, could you maybe think about helping Jessie go to college?"

He put his hand out and brushed at my hair. "You bet I would, and H.J., you'd be my partner." His voice got sort of soft. "Never had a son, but you've took the place. You'd be a partner and inherit it all someday."

"So," I said, "if I needed a good bit of money for

something special, something that meant a whole bunch to me, there might be a way I could work for it?"

Uncle Delbert rested against the back of the chair again. I wasn't certain that he was listening, but then he said, "Sure, son, whatever you need."

Neither one of us talked for a while. Uncle Delbert kept his eyes closed and his head back. I just pulled up blades of grass. I guess we were both thinking. He was studying on how to handle the deal with Mr. Summers. I was lost in plans to rescue Lucky.

First I would need a cage, and it would have to be strong. I could build one, I was sure. There was still some lumber stacked behind the restaurant left from building the court. I'd take some of that, say I was going to build a tree house or something.

I could rig a sort of trap, using food for bait. Maybe I could get the cat in the cage, but then what? I'd have to get Lucky somewhere safe.

I glanced over at Uncle Delbert and an idea hit me. "You been down in eastern Oklahoma, ain't you?" I asked. "Didn't you say there's mountains down there?"

He straightened up and looked kind of surprised to see me. "What?" he said.

"I was wondering about how it is in the eastern part of the state."

"Pretty. Nice little mountains and lots of streams."

"Many people live up in them mountains?"

"There's places you could walk for days, not see a soul. Why?"

I shrugged. "Just wondering. Guess I'd like to see some place like that."

"Tell you what, H.J., we just might take us a fishing trip down there, you and me. When things is settled around here we might just load up the truck and take off."

I shot out of my chair. "That'd be great. Real great." I was sure I could talk Uncle Delbert into helping me. There would be a way to save Lucky. A robin in the tree above us broke into a song. I grinned up at him, thinking he was on my side.

Uncle Delbert seemed to forget me again. He stared at some ants that were building a little hill near his feet. "Don't never want to be like them ants, boy," he said softly. "Just a-following the same old track in and out, back and forth, day in and day out. They ain't got vision, H.J. Just work till they die."

I didn't know how to answer him. Mr. Whipple said we ought to admire ants, working hard and steady. But when I looked up at Uncle Delbert, I could see he didn't really expect an answer.

"Guess I'd better go see when Mama and Jessie want to leave," I said.

I hadn't got all the way up, when Uncle Delbert grabbed my arm. "I'm going over to the bank." He squeezed my arm. "Maybell knows I've got to go to town for supplies. I can just stop at the bank, sign the papers, and have the cash waiting when Summers comes back." He nodded his head over and over, and he smiled. "Run on," he said, and I did.

It felt good to race across the grass and past the blinking Deluxe Tourist Court sign. On the steps of the restaurant, I tried to tone down the smile that I knew showed all over my face.

Aunt Maybell must have had dinner pretty much ready because she was at one of the tables with Mama and Jessie. They had Coca-Cola in glasses with ice in them.

Aunt Maybell asked if I wanted a glass, but I shook my head. I liked my Coca-Cola from the little round bottles straight from the soda pop box, but I was too excited to want any at all.

I moved a little past them before I said anything because I didn't want Mama to see my face. "I was wondering if maybe I could get me some of that leftover lumber out back," I said. "Me and Buddy are fixing to build us a real swank tree house."

"Take it," said Aunt Maybell. "Needs to be hauled off anyway."

I scooted on out into the kitchen before anyone could ask questions. Then I went to work. First I took the tin bucket of scraps from the floor by the sink and toted it real careful to the truck. It fit just right in the corner between a tire and an old battery.

At the lumber pile, I let out a little whoop of joy. The boards were just the right length, wouldn't even have to be cut for the cage. I ran my hand along the smooth side of the first piece I picked up. "Things sure are working out, Lucky," I whispered. "They're working out for you and for my sister." I could imagine his yellow eyes looking at me.

It didn't take long to pile the lumber all around the bucket so that no one could see it. It was good that I worked quick because just as I put the last board in, Mama and Jessie showed up, ready to go.

We got in the truck, but Uncle Delbert walked over to stand by Jessie's window and talk to her. "Still got a hankering to go to college?" he asked.

Jessie nodded, and I could see the terrible wanting on her face.

"Who knows," Uncle Delbert said. "Could be a way might make its way plain." He smiled real big.

I wanted to bounce on the old truck seat and clap my hands. Mama looked worried. "Start the truck," she said.

Just as I had the engine fired up, Aunt Maybell rushed out the front door of the restaurant.

She was waving her arms. "Thank the Lord you're not gone," she shouted, and she hurried over to my window.

Everyone got quiet, waiting to hear what she was so excited about. "Ya'll had just went out the door when the telephone rung. Guy wanting to reserve four cabins."

"Good deal," said Uncle Delbert.

"Yes, but get this." Aunt Maybell paused to catch her breath from the rush. "The fellow is working for the zoo. A bunch of them is coming out here. Said they've checked pretty much everywhere else. They think maybe that escaped cat is in these parts."

"Gosh," I said, like I was real shocked.

Mama and Jessie were trying to talk too, but Aunt Maybell broke in. "I wanted you to know on account of talking about building tree houses and being in pastures and all." She put her hand on my arm and squeezed her message to me.

"All that's out now," Mama said from beside me.

"The tree's in Buddy's yard," I lied.

"Well, you just stay out of pastures," Aunt Maybell said.

Uncle Delbert started talking about how he hoped Papa made it home soon and saying we ought to keep our stock up.

I wasn't listening. All I could seem to hear was the heavy thumping of my heart.

7

ALL THE WAY HOME, I took turns thinking about Lucky and nearly busting with wanting to tell Jessie that Uncle Delbert was going to make lots of money. But when we drove up into our yard, my mind skipped to Ring, because no big black dog ran down the red-dirt driveway to meet us.

I squinted my eyes, trying to see out beyond the barn into the pasture. We came rattling to a stop, but still he wasn't there.

"Wonder where Ring is," I said to Mama and Jessie as we climbed out, but I didn't wait for an answer, just started off toward the barn. "Come here, Ring," I called. "Come here. Come here, boy."

I strained, listening for his answering bark, but all I heard was Mama. "Don't you go looking for that dog, H.J." She was about to go into the house, and she called out to me right before she opened the screen. The door slammed behind her. Then she stuck her head back out. "I mean it," she yelled.

I sort of waved at Mama, but I didn't make any promises. If Ring was gone, I'd go looking for him. I'd have to.

Jessie stood out by the fence, moving her head to see up and down the dusty road. I walked out to be beside her. "He's always home," I said. "Don't leave the place without me."

Jessie started calling, too, and I could see from her face that she was worried. After a while she put her hand on my arm. "Are you thinking he might have gotten mixed up with that leopard?"

"It's an awful big cat," I said. "One slap from that powerful paw could knock Ring down."

"H.J.," she said, "have you seen that leopard?" I could feel her looking right at me, and I didn't want to lie.

Then a way out came to me. "I seen that same cat. Remember? When Papa worked up at the zoo for the WPA."

She sort of tugged at my arm. "Let's go on in. He might show up before we finish eating. I sure can't go back to town with Ring missing."

I walked beside her toward the house, but on the porch we both turned to look once more for a glimpse of black ears or a tail with a white ring.

Jessie held the door, and I followed her on inside. My stomach had been growling on the way home, but at the table I didn't want a bite. Mama had food already in my plate, but I could only eat one boiled egg and a bite or two of beans, even though I usually like them better when they're left from the day before.

Pictures of Ring and Lucky kept going through my mind. I could imagine Ring running up to him. The cat would snarl and whirl with its great claws, or maybe the leopard would be in a tree. Ring might not even see it until it was too late. And it would all be my fault. If I had told someone, Lucky would be back in the zoo by now.

Jessie left the table to go over to look out the window. "You two quit fretting over that dog and eat," Mama said. "He can take care of hisself."

Just then I quit hearing Mama because of the most wonderful sound. Ring was barking. Out by the back porch, Ring barked up a storm. Jessie and me both got up and ran for the door. Mama said something about finishing our food, but she didn't say it very strong.

Ring jumped around wagging his tail when he saw us like he knew we had been worried about him. Jessie perched on the step and put her arm around his neck. "You're the best old dog in the world," she said. I got on the other side, stroking his back.

After Jessie went inside, I drifted on out to the stock pen to check on the level in the water tank. I sort of liked taking care of the stock while Papa was gone, doing a man's job and all. What I really liked, though, was shoving my arms in that cool water all the way up to my elbows. On hot days it was a pure delight. The sides of the tank felt all soft from the green mossy scum that grew there.

I straightened, dripping water, when I heard a noise on the road. Two strange pickups rattled by, throwing up dust.

Both trucks had men in the front seat, and I saw the barrels of rifles, sticking up from the space between the men.

By the time I got to the fence, there was nothing left but red dirt-clouds for me to stare after. I clenched my fists and wanted to chase after them. "He ain't here," I might yell. Or maybe I could threaten them, tell them not to set one stinking foot on our land. But there wasn't no use.

With determination I moved back across the grass toward the house. Lies or threats wouldn't help, but maybe I could still save Lucky. Maybe he was *lucky* to have made my acquaintance.

From the front steps I could see the lumber, still in the truck. The first thing was to get that cage built. I straightened my shoulders and opened the door.

Mama and Jessie had the blue flowered material across the kitchen table, and they both had scissors. I didn't go all the way into the room, just stood in the door. "Is it OK for me to take the lumber over to Buddy's?"

Mama looked up at me. "That truck could break down. I don't want you out there by yourself."

"It's only a mile to Buddy's. The truck run good this morning. Besides, that cat wouldn't be walking down a road."

"That's right," Jessie said. She walked over to look out the window. "If he's out there, I bet he's hiding."

"Sure," I said. "Hiding all scared to death of going back to that cement pen."

My voice must have sounded too interested or something. Jessie and Mama were both looking at me. "Well," I said. "I saw that leopard once. I feel sorry for it, that's all."

"Go on then," said Mama, but she pointed at me with her scissors. "You just don't be taking any foolish chances, you hear me."

I nodded and headed for the door. Jessie followed me. "Howard and his folks are bound to come by for me before you get back," she said. She kept walking with me. I sure didn't want Jessie to get close enough to the back of the truck to spot the bucket of scraps, so I stopped by the pump.

"See you next time, then," I said, but I could see she wanted to say something. She put her hand on my arm.

I looked down at the toe of my boot. If Jessie asked me straight out if I'd seen the leopard off in the pasture, what could I say?

She made a little sound, clearing her throat before she talked. "I was thinking about Uncle Delbert's comment, you know, about something coming along so I could go to school. And about how you said Uncle Delbert might make some money and decide to help me. What does it mean?"

It was a relief that she wasn't asking about Lucky, but still the answer didn't come easy. "It's sort of a secret," I said. "Something I ain't supposed to talk about." I heard her sort of draw in her breath, and I had to say something more. "I believe it'll happen," I added. "I just got a hunch good things might come to you."

Jessie started to whirl, her hair and skirt standing out in the breeze. It made me feel awful good to see her so happy, but I was scared she'd crash into the pump. I reached out and grabbed her arm. "Hey," I said, "slow down."

All out of breath, she leaned against the pump and ran her hand up and down the handle. "Oh, I'll pay Uncle Delbert back when I'm a vet. I swear, and help Papa buy things for the farm, and Mama nice dresses and pretty bowls." She laughed. "And you, H.J. I'll help you go to college or do whatever it is you want."

"There's just one thing I want, but it can't wait till you're done with school." Right off, I was sorry for talking, and I looked toward the truck, wishing I could just run for it.

"What?" She took my arm again and gripped hard. I shook my head to show I didn't aim to say.

"It's that big cat, isn't it? You're hating to see it caught." I didn't answer, but Jessie saw. "I know how you feel, but you have to promise me you won't take any chances if you should see that animal. There's nothing you can do."

I wanted to blurt out the truth about Lucky and beg her to help me. I didn't, though. Jessie would get worked up about me getting hurt. "I got to go." I pulled away and hurried toward the truck.

"H.J.," she called, and I looked back at her over my shoulder. "When I'm a vet," she said, "and you're all grown up, maybe we can do something for creatures like that leopard. Maybe we can work together on it then."

Without an answer, I slid behind the wheel, but before I closed the door I yelled back to my sister. "Call Ring," I shouted over the sound of the engine. "Just in case he might run after me."

When I drove off, I saw Jessie and Ring playing tug-of-war with a stick. It was his favorite game, and I knew he would be happy to stay home.

I was glad the gate to the south pasture was over a little rise just out of sight of the house. I jumped out, let down the wire fence, and coaxed the old truck up the little hill and as close to the trees as I could park.

It took me a while to get the lumber out of the truck.

All the time I was reaching, stacking, and carrying, I kept glancing toward the trees searching for a glimpse of Lucky. I listened too, listened for the terrible sound of pickups on dirt roads.

Sweat ran down my face, but I didn't take a minute's rest between unloading the lumber and getting three loads over to the little clearing in the trees.

I dropped on my knees beside the pile of boards and reached for my hammer. Building the cage didn't take as long as I figured. Things were moving pretty good when I hit my thumb. I yelled, "Dang," real loud, but I didn't even take a minute to stick it in my mouth. The lumber was perfect, two-by-fours for the frame and plenty of scraps for the sides. I put in lots of nails to make it strong and spaced the wood so there would be air.

All the time I worked, birds made music in the trees. Their songs lifted my spirits, and with every pound of my hammer I said a little prayer.

Rigging the trap door was hardest. I wished for Papa to help. "I'm going to buy him," I said aloud, thinking about my father. I knew Papa wouldn't hold with me taking a leopard that didn't belong to me. A story in the paper said that the zoo had paid three hundred dollars for Lucky. I smiled. Thank heavens for Uncle Delbert and his vision.

After I hammered the last nail, I filled the old dish-pan I had thrown in with Aunt Maybell's scraps and set it at the back. When the cat touched the pan, a board would fall and close the door.

I folded my arms and stood back to admire the cage. "Come on, Lucky," I whispered. "Come on and let me help you."

Suddenly I realized that the birds had quit singing. The pasture was totally quiet. Even the breeze was still. He's out there, I thought. Lucky's out there, watching. I ignored the leftover lumber, grabbed up my hammer, and walked backward to the truck. I hated shattering the quiet by starting the old engine.

8

BACK HOME, I SLIPPED in to get a drink from the water
bucket, but Mama heard me. She sent me out to the barn
to carry up a big old box of fruit jars and told me to start
washing them out. Canning time was way off. Mama
knew something was up, and she wanted to keep me
busy. She had one eye on me most of the time, but every
time I could I stepped out to watch and listen, wondering
what was going on with Lucky. I imagined him stretched
out on a tree branch, and I prayed the hunters would stay
far away.

It was getting on toward evening when I heard all the
barking and ran to the door. A pickup with men in the
front and dogs in the back pulled into our driveway. Ring
was having a fit.

Mama came to stand beside me. "Mercy," she said.
"They must be the zoo fellows."

My heart was racing faster than the engine on their
big pickup. One of the men got out and walked to the
door.

"How do you do, ma'am," he said to Mama when he was close to the porch. "I'm Charlie Davis. We're looking for the escaped leopard, and we'd like permission to go on your land."

"No," I blurted out. "You might shoot our livestock."

"Hush, H.J.," Mama said. "You know the stock's shut up."

"Well, then," Mr. Davis asked, "do we have your OK?"

"I'd have to go along." I tried again. "Make sure no fences get damaged and to show you what land's ours."

Mr. Davis nodded. "There's a group of local men." He pointed with his head down the road. "They're waiting for us. Glad to have you join if your mother doesn't object."

I stepped toward him, but Mama put out her hand to stop me. "I'd want him to stay back," she said. "Not to get near the cat or in the way of fire."

"It's an organized hunt, ma'am. No one will be hurt." He looked at me. "We'd rather you didn't bring your gun, son. Told another boy just about your age the same thing."

Buddy, I thought. Buddy's bound to be down there. My legs felt shaky. "That's just fine, sir. I ain't wanting to do no shooting."

"H.J.," Mama called as we walked down the steps. "You use your head."

I looked back at her and waved. I'm sure trying to use my head, I thought. I'm trying harder than I ever did try.

When we were down the steps, I stopped. "I'll drive our truck," I told Mr. Davis, "and lead the way." I pointed off to the north. "Best place to start would be the north pasture." I half expected Mama to come running out and shout that I shouldn't take the truck, but she didn't.

Still I hurried out the driveway just in case. Like Mr. Davis said, men waited for us, two pickup loads on the main road. In the back of the second truck, I saw Buddy. He grinned and waved real big from the side of the bed, and I could see a stack of guns.

At the entrance to the north pasture, I stopped. I'd get out, open the gate, and let the others drive in first. I might want out fast. I motioned to Mr. Davis. "Drive on in," I shouted. "Right on up to the trees." I got back in to follow the last truck.

They were organizing by the time I stopped. Buddy came running toward me. "Hurry," he yelled. I didn't move from behind the wheel, but Buddy came right over and jerked open the door. "Get out." He kept glancing over his shoulder at the men who were grabbing guns from the pickup bed.

I slid to the ground, but I left the door open in case I wanted back in quick. My hand gripped the handle like I was afraid Buddy might try to drag me.

"Come on." He reached out to yank at my arm, but I pulled away. "What's wrong with you? You're fixing to mess around till we miss the whole thing."

"Ain't going. Don't want to hunt no leopard."

"H.J., this is big, the biggest thing we ever had a crack at. They might even give out a reward or something."

Rage rose up in me. "Cripes," I growled. "You make me sick, wanting money for chasing some scared animal."

Shock swept over Buddy's face and left his mouth open. The hurt in his eyes irritated me even more, and with one quick lunge I shoved him. "Go on," I said. "Run join the mighty hunters."

He stumbled, but he didn't fall. Straightening up, he gave me one long look. "You'll be sorry," he said before he turned to race across the grass toward the others.

For a second it flashed through my mind to wonder if Buddy meant I'd be sorry for pushing him or that I'd be sorry for missing the hunt. Then Mr. Davis started to point and shout orders. "You guys spread out and take that direction. Walk to the fence. If you see the cat, fire three shots."

"Don't shoot the animal, though," one of the men added, and his voice got even louder. "Don't shoot Lucky unless there's real danger."

"Sure, Marvin," said Mr. Davis. "We'll try to get

him alive, but we've got to shoot if it looks like he's getting away. This hunt's gone on long enough."

There were sounds of agreement from the other men. I studied the one called Marvin, and I knew he was the Mr. Andrews who had been quoted in the paper, the one who had named Lucky and who cared for him.

Pushing by some guys with guns, I moved toward the man and stopped right beside him. His boots were brown, with big thick soles. I wanted to keep staring down at them, but Papa always said to look people in the eyes, so I tried. But Marvin Andrews wasn't interested in me. He gazed over my head toward the trees, searching.

On purpose, I sort of bumped against him. "Sorry," I muttered, and when he glanced my way I added, "I hope he don't get shot."

Mr. Andrews gave me a sort of sad little smile. "I do too, son. I most surely do." He moved off to join the others, who were splitting into groups. For a minute I thought of running after him and telling him my plan, but I knew it was useless. He couldn't help me steal the zoo's leopard.

As the men moved by me, their grins made me want to clench my fists. But I stood still, barely breathing. No one seemed to notice I wasn't taking part.

With guns held high, the hunters disappeared among the trees. Buddy marched along with them like a big shot, and he never even turned his head my way. The sun was going down fast, and from the length of the shadows around me, I figured it must be almost dark in the woods. I took a step to follow after the others, but I stopped.

There was nothing I could do in this spot. If Lucky waited out there where the searchers stalked him, I couldn't do him any good. For sure I didn't want to stand around watching as they dragged him out in nets or even worse, maybe end up seeing his powerful body all broken and lifeless.

In one quick motion, I whirled and ran to the truck, throwing my body into the open door without slowing my pace. "Start," I said. My foot pumped hard on the gas. "Start quick," and it roared into action.

At the south pasture, I jerked the gate hard and broke the wire fastener, but I let the wires fall unnoticed to the ground. With the stock in the cow lot, the fence was unimportant. I drove the truck close to the trees, cut the engine, and hopped out, leaving the door open.

When my feet hit the ground, though, I made myself slow down instead of charging into the woods. Lucky could be crouched in a tree. I wished for a light, and I stepped slowly toward the big cottonwood tree.

When I was close to the huge trunk, I put out my hand to run my fingers over the bark. Then I made myself lift my foot to move forward. What I saw made me cry out, but it was a cry for joy. Lucky was there, caught in that cage. His spotted tail stuck plain as anything through the slats.

"Golly," I whispered. "I done it. I really done it." No answering sound came from the pen, and I inched toward him. It was almost dark by now, and his fiery eyes stared out at me.

I edged closer, expecting him to growl or hiss, but he didn't. I had underestimated Lucky's size, and I could see that the pen was not tall enough for him to stand on all fours. He hunched miserable and defeated like.

I blinked back tears. "Just you wait," I stammered, "I swear it ain't going to be long before you're running free." I bent close to the wooden cell, and I put out my hand to touch the slats, but I pulled it back. Lucky could shoot his paw through if he decided to, and his claws could make my hand look like a shredded piece of rag.

Stepping back, I studied the cage. I would have to move it by pushing on the back and the side where the wood was solid.

The urgent bay of hounds on a trail came through the trees from the north pasture. "They've picked up a scent," I said, and my heart raced even faster than ever before. The cage had to get moved, had to be hidden.

Barely remembering to be careful where my hands went, I threw my weight against the pen. It slid on the grass, but only a few inches. I had not expected to have to move Lucky in a hurry, and I had not realized how big the great cat really was. Again I shoved, holding my breath and bulging my eyes with the strain. Encouraged by a slight movement, I pushed until I had to collapse on the grass behind the cage, but I stayed down just the second it took to pull more breath into my burning lungs.

No time for resting. I jerked myself up and studied the situation. Getting the cage to the pickup at this rate was not going to happen, not in time. Even if I did, how would I ever lift Lucky into the truck?

The sound of engines floated through the trees from the road. Frantic, I streaked to the edge of the woods for a look. What I saw was a great relief. The Cadillac. Mr. Summers's shiny Cadillac pulled off the road just down from the pasture gate where I had left the fence down. At just about the same second a blue Ford came from the other direction, and it stopped too.

The Ford seemed familiar, but I couldn't think where I had seen it until the driver got out and walked toward the Cadillac. He was a real tall man and skinny too. Jamison, the fellow whose wife had made him back out of the oil deal.

It crossed my mind to wonder what the two men were doing out on country roads, but I sure didn't dwell on it. Two strong men were nearby. They were not hunters, and one of them was a friend of my uncle Delbert's, had even let me drive his car.

Help was near. I took time to pull in a deep breath, then flung myself out of the woods toward the Cadillac. I wanted to cry out, but there wasn't wind left in me for a yell. I ran silently, smiling because everything would be all right. I would say I was driving the cat to the zoo men, or I would say I had bought it. I wasn't sure what claim to make, but something would come to me. These men had been sent to us. Me and the cat were both lucky.

I was out the gate and close enough to see what was going on in the Cadillac where Mr. Jamison had joined Mr. Summers, who was counting out bills. A big stack of green money was on the dashboard. Again I wondered what was going on, but their business didn't matter. I was beside the car, throwing myself to rest against the hood. "Help," I cried. "Mr. Summers, you got to help me."

Both men jumped from the car. "What are you doing here, kid?" Mr. Summers was not smiling, and his voice had lost its friendly tone.

He doesn't recognize me, I thought. "I'm Delbert's nephew. Remember?"

Mr. Jamison stepped around the car, and grabbed at my arm. "Who set you spying on us?" he demanded.

"No," I said. "Listen, please. I need help lifting something."

"Beat it, kid. We've got business," Mr. Summers growled.

I jerked my arm away from Jamison, and unbelieving, I turned from one hard face to the other. "Please," I said, but Mr. Summers motioned me away.

"It'd only take a minute," I pleaded.

Mr. Jamison shook his fist at me. "Want me to show you what no means?" he shouted.

I turned and ran back through the pasture gate. Just before I reached the truck, I heard the engines start, and looking back, I saw both cars drive away, fast.

Something was wrong. Ralph Summers was not the man he had pretended to be at the Deluxe Tourist Court, and I knew things did not look good for Uncle Delbert and his dream. I could not dwell on the subject, though. From the trees came Lucky's cry. It was not a growl, more cough like, but the cough was a sad one, pitiful and dripping with misery.

Passing the truck, I happened to notice a rope in the back. Maybe I could tie the rope to the cage, then pull with the truck. Of course, I couldn't get the cage any closer to the truck than the length of the rope, but at least it would be in the clearing.

I might think of something else. I grabbed the rope and made for the cage. Standing above the pen, I tried to figure how to get the rope in one side of the cage and out the other without sticking in my hand.

Then I heard them. The dogs were coming near. I could even catch the shouts of the men. "This way," one yelled. "They're on to him now."

"No," I whispered, and I moved between the cage and the road. I spread out my legs and stretched my arms up and out, like I could stop the dogs and stop a dozen or more men with guns.

It won't work, I told myself, and I wanted to crumple to the ground to cry on the grass. Instead, I turned once more to meet Lucky's eyes. I knew what I had to do. I would open the cage. There was nothing else to do. Trapped in the prison I had made, he wouldn't have even a little chance. If I opened the gate, he could escape.

"What if he jumps you?" I wondered aloud, but I shrugged my shoulders. A tree limb, long and thin, caught my eye. Perfect! I grabbed it. Using the limb as a tool, I could move the front latch while standing toward the back of the cage. Maybe Lucky would run straight out and away. Maybe he would not turn back to attack the person who had trapped him.

My hands shook, but still I guided the stick to the latch and pushed it down. The door fell open, and I sucked in my breath, waiting. Lucky did not move.

In my mind I urged him to go. Run, I pleaded. You're free. Afraid to make a sound, I stood silent, begging the huge cat to crawl out of the cage and to escape. He stayed hunched into a miserable knot. Maybe he's been too cramped to move, I thought.

I could hear feet now, running. The hunters moved toward us. I could almost feel their breath, hot and de-

131

termined. Then I heard someone call my name. "H.J., H.J., where are you?"

Relief washed over me like cool stream water. It was Papa. My papa was out there, and everything would turn out all right.

In the shadowy trees, the hunters who first broke into the clearing looked like gray giants. Desperate to spot my father, I glanced madly from one dark form to another. Papa would save Lucky. He had to.

Then I saw him. "H.J.," he called. "Son, are you all right?" I turned to run to him. Like I was little again, I wanted to have him wrap me in his arms, lift me up high.

I had almost reached Papa when someone shouted. "Look. The cat. He's right there."

I whirled back to see Lucky, out of the cage and running, running away from us all toward the trees at the other side of the clearing. "Go," I screamed. "Run, Lucky, run."

My words were drowned out by the shots, two quick blasts through the dark. Lucky was moving so fast he looked like his feet did not touch the ground, but the bullets brought him down.

His great body rippled to the earth, the muscles and spotted skin folding together into one wretched pile.

Someone hollered, "It was me. I got him." I didn't turn toward the voice, but I was pretty sure it was Buddy's father.

Instead of running to my father, I changed my direction and ran to Lucky's broken body. "No," I screamed, and I dropped to stroke the soft, warm fur.

It was Mr. Andrews who lifted me up. I could hear his words. "Sorry, boy," but somehow I didn't quite realize he was talking to me.

Papa was beside me then. He did pull me into his arms. "He was made to be free," I said. "Just wild and running free." Then I started to cry. In front of them all I bawled like a five-year-old.

9

I DON'T EVEN REMEMBER MUCH about going back to our place with Papa, just that sometime between leaving Lucky and climbing our front steps, I stopped sobbing.

Papa's jobs for the WPA were all over, so he was home to stay. Once that would have made me so happy, but now there wasn't space inside me for glad feelings.

Instead of going into the house, I dropped on the porch and let my legs rest on the steps. Mama came out, and I was afraid she'd set me off to crying again, but she only bent down to brush back my hair from off my forehead. Her hand felt nice and cool, but it pleased me that Mama and Papa both went on in and left me alone.

Ring came and stuck his head against my shoulder. We stayed there way into the night, me looking at the stars and listening to the owl down by the barn. Finally, thunder started in the west and rain made me go inside.

Next morning Mama came into my room real soft, but I was already awake, just staring up at the ceiling.

"You could stay home today," she said. "Wouldn't be out of the way none, bound to be tuckered."

I got up, though, and I hurried to get off to school. Not stopping at Buddy's, I went right straight to the bridge. I moved the rock, dropped down, stuck my hands in the soft red dirt, and started digging for the clapper.

Nothing warned me that Buddy was coming, but just about when my hand touched the metal, I looked up to see his overalls legs in front of me. "I'd of helped you, H.J.," he said, and there was misery in his voice. "Didn't you see that I'd of helped you if I'd of knowed how much you cared about that cat?"

I looked up at him then, saw his face all earnest, and the bad feelings went out of me. There wasn't no use blaming Buddy or even his father for being the one to shoot Lucky. There wasn't nothing left in me for being mad any more than there was for being glad.

I tried to smile at him. "Thanks," I said, "but I expect things couldn't have turned out much different."

"Why you digging up the clapper?" He hunkered down beside me.

"Just not in the mood for a joke right now," I said. I saw the disappointed look in his eyes. "We'll think of something even better later," I promised, but we both knew it wasn't true.

We didn't talk on the rest of the way to school.

Mr. Whipple was standing out by the steps. I walked right up to him and held out the clapper. "Here," I said, "I took this."

"Me too," Buddy put in real fast. "I got the licks coming too."

Mr. Whipple looked down at the piece in his hand. There was still red mud on it. "How nice you found the clapper, Hobert," he said.

I stared at him. "No," I said. "I took it."

He nodded and smiled at me. "You've learned a good deal lately. I think we might go so far as to say you've become a man." Then he turned away. "Time for school," he shouted out over the playground. "Our bell is temporarily out of commission."

As soon as we were in our places, another strange thing happened. Jewel Tea poked my shoulder from her seat behind me. When I turned around, she held out a piece of paper torn from her Big Chief tablet.

It was folded, and she watched me as I opened it to read, "H.J., I'm real sorry about what happened to that leopard. I wish he could have lived and run free. Your friend, J.T."

I looked up at Jewel Tea. She had a sort of sad little smile on her face. I could see she meant what she wrote. I smiled back at her. For the first time since Lucky died I felt something, and what I felt was friendship for Jewel Tea. I didn't figure I'd ever want to torment her again. "Thanks," I whispered.

After school, I went right home. I wondered what was going on at the Deluxe Tourist Court, but I just didn't have it in me to go over there and see. I found out anyhow, and the news was not good.

The sheriff came to our door to ask if I'd noticed anything about Mr. Summers that Aunt Maybell and Uncle Delbert hadn't. Papa talked to him first, out on the porch, but after he told the sheriff what I'd seen in the woods, they called me to repeat the story.

When I got to the part about how they counted money, the sheriff said, "Dividing the loot." I leaned against the porch rail, feeling like I might puke.

Summers, we learned, was not the man's name at all. Seems he was wanted in Texas for the same kind of cheating folks out of money. So was his partner, the one called Jamison.

I stood there, listening to the sheriff and gripping the porch rail. Remembering how I'd admired Summers made me sick. I thought about how he had acted when the phone call came, like he was afraid something had happened to his wife. There wasn't any wife, the sheriff said, and the phone call was a hook to pull Uncle Delbert in on Mr. Summers's crooked fishing line.

When the sheriff left, Papa and me stayed on the porch watching him drive off. I thought Papa would carry on about how foolish Uncle Delbert had been to give up his land for the court and how his dreaming ended up costing him everything.

He didn't, though. He put his arm around me. "World's full of hurting, son," he said, "but we'll get through it."

Of course, Uncle Delbert and Aunt Maybell couldn't make the payments on the loan against their place, and they had to move out of the Deluxe Tourist Court. I helped them pack up their things. In the kitchen I wrapped up the blue graniteware pots in newspapers, so they wouldn't bump against the thick white plates.

There were spots in the newspaper where things had been cut out. Aunt Maybell saw me looking at the holes. "I saved all the stories about the leopard," she said, real soft. "Thought you might want them."

"Someday," I said, "I guess I'd like to have them."

Out in front, I traced the capital D and E of the sign with my finger, and I suggested to Uncle Delbert that we load it into the back of the truck. "No real use," he said, but I talked him into it, saying he might open up another place one of these days.

"You're like my grandpappy," he said as we carried the sign between us. "Grandpappy always said, 'Save your Confederate money. The South will rise again.'"

Mama held our front screen door open for Aunt Maybell and Uncle Delbert. "This was your mama's house," she said, and she touched Aunt Maybell's hand. "It's right, you living here."

Papa said how glad he was to have them, and he settled on the bench at supper, giving Uncle Delbert his chair.

For a day or so it was pretty quiet around our place. Then one morning Aunt Maybell announced, "I'm done moping. Ain't none of us lame. Ain't none of us sick with fever. We been down before. It'll all come out in the wash." She patted Uncle Delbert's shoulder, and I watched his face perk up. He still didn't have much to say around Papa, though.

It was just about dark one evening after supper, when me and Uncle Delbert settled down on the front porch. A pickup pulled into the driveway. Ring took to barking and Papa came out to see what the ruckus was.

When Mr. Andrews from the zoo got out, I sucked in my breath.

He walked right up to the steps. Papa went to the edge of the porch and called out, "Howdy," but it was me Mr. Andrews looked at when he climbed the steps and started talking.

"You're the boy, aren't you? The one who tried to help Lucky."

I nodded my head, and I stood up. This time it wasn't hard to look Mr. Andrews in the eye. He was coming right toward me, holding out his hand. "I been thinking about you," he said. "Wanted to say thank you and to tell you there will be a job for you at the zoo if you ever want it, when you're a little older."

Papa spoke up before I had a chance. "Real nice of you, coming all the way out here. Set down, won't you?" He pulled a rocker away from the wall.

I had other ideas, though. "Could you and me maybe go for a little walk?" I blurted the words out quick.

"Sure." Mr. Andrews turned back toward the steps, and I went with him, setting a good pace and not looking at all in Papa's direction.

"I liked that leopard a whole bunch," I told him as we moved.

"So did I." He put his hand on my shoulder for a minute. "I see lots of animals in my work, but some just get to be special."

We were near the stock tank by then. I went over and plunged my hand down into the cool water, touched the soft green sides, and started talking. "The zoo? Is there a college near there?"

"Not far," he said. "Are you thinking maybe you'll go to college someday?" He sounded interested, and my hopes started flying high.

"My sister." I shook the water from my hands and faced him. "Jessie's her name, and she wants to be a veterinarian, wants it more than anything. There ain't money for school."

Mr. Andrews put his own hands into the tank before he spoke. "A vet, huh? It's a spunky ambition for a girl."

"Jessie's spunky all right. You should have seen her taking care of our dog when he got bit by a snake." Ring had followed us, and Mr. Andrews looked down at him.

"Looks pretty healthy now," he said.

I didn't want to talk about Ring. "Can you help her? You know, instead of saving a job for me?"

He rubbed his wet hands across his face and then kind of stroked his chin. "My wife would take to a girl like that, sort of wanted to go into the field herself once."

"You'll help her then?" I tried not to yell the question.

He grinned at me. "Pretty important to you, isn't it?" Before I could answer, he went on. "I don't see why not." He took a little pad and a pencil from the pocket of his khaki shirt. "Here's my name and address, phone number too. You tell your sister to give me a call. I'll see that there's a job, and Mrs. Andrews will help with a place to live. Wouldn't surprise me if Margaret doesn't decide to put her up right at our place."

I wanted to throw my arms around him, but I took the paper, slipped it into my overalls, and grabbed his hand. "You won't be sorry," I told him. "Jessie works real hard." I held firm as I shook his hand.

"Glad I came," he said. "Something told me to."

We started back to the house then. Papa and Uncle Delbert were still on the porch, waiting.

Mr. Andrews didn't slow down much as we walked toward his truck. "I'll talk to your father. Tell him how my wife will watch over your sister."

Papa. What if he out and out refused Mr. Andrews's offer? Close to the pickup, I stopped and put my hand out to touch the fender. "Maybe it would be best if your wife sort of wrote a letter or something." I used my head to point at the porch. "See, it might take him a little time, getting used to the idea."

He nodded. "I see. Guess I'll be on my way then." He opened the pickup door. When he was on the running board, he waved his hat and called out to Papa and Uncle Delbert. "Come up to the zoo and see us. You're welcome anytime."

"Thank you," I said. "I just thank you so much."

He was settled behind the wheel. "It's good to see a young man so concerned about his sister." He smiled at me. "You and I'll work on this together like we didn't get to with Lucky."

I watched him drive away, then squared my shoulders and headed toward the porch.

"Should have asked the man to set for a while," Papa said.

I swallowed hard and plunged right in. "He's going

to give Jessie a job at the zoo. Said his wife would help her get settled up there so she can go to college."

In a streak Papa was up and over at the steps like he might run after Mr. Andrews, but there was nothing left in our driveway except the dust his truck had stirred up.

"He's gone, Hobert," said Uncle Delbert. "And Jessie'll be gone too before long, off to college." He was still in his chair, but he had his arms folded across his chest. He spoke up real determined. "Jessie ought to have her chance. Lord knows an education couldn't hurt nobody. If I'd of had me one, that devil Summers wouldn't of put me here sponging off family."

"You're welcome in my house," said Papa. "Ain't I made you welcome?"

Papa had turned to Uncle Delbert and they were staring at each other. I stayed back a ways, knowing the strain between them was fixing to come out in the open.

"You have sure enough been good to me, Hobert. Just like you was good to that Riley fellow and his family at Christmas. You ain't the kind to kick a man when he is down. What I'm a-wondering, though, is if you'd have been so good had I made me a go of my business?" Uncle Delbert breathed out deep and stuck out his chin. "Just suppose you'd of been wrong about me selling my land. What if I'd made me some money, would you still be offering me a place at your table? Or would you just have quit inviting me to eat altogether?"

144

I waited, half afraid that Papa might walk over, latch on to the front of Uncle Delbert's overalls, jerk him up out of the chair, and whomp him one. I didn't figure my papa would ever hit a man who wasn't standing up.

Papa didn't move, though. He quit glaring at Uncle Delbert, and he took to looking at the boards on the porch floor. Nobody said a word for a long time. It was me that finally talked. "So," I said. "Is it OK with you, Papa, for me to give Jessie this paper with how to get hold of Mr. Andrews?"

He nodded his head. "I'll not hinder your sister's dream," he said. Then he looked up at Uncle Delbert. "Wasn't you thinking once about planting peanuts? Maybe you and me could put in a few, have a little cash crop to help out Jessie some."

Uncle Delbert went right into the wonders of peanuts. I just listened. It wasn't long before they got off on politics. Papa lambasted the Republicans, and Uncle Delbert hollered that Roosevelt wasn't the savior Papa thought he was.

I liked listening to them, but I wanted to go in and put the note in the chiffonier drawer for Jessie. She was coming home in a day or two, and I kept imagining how her face would look when I told her about the offer.

I was just pushing the drawer closed when Aunt Maybell stuck her head in at the door. "I put them newspaper articles in your room," she said. "You know, the ones about the cat."

"Thanks." I went on in there, and they were on my bed, pieces of newspaper with Lucky's picture. I dropped down to my knees beside the bed. Lucky stared up at me. I smoothed the articles against the quilt, and studied the great cat. "You were a lot bigger in real life," I whispered. "A whole lot bigger."

I got up, took the papers, and laid them real careful like between the pages of *Tom Sawyer*. I went out back then and stood on the porch. Ring came up, wagging his tail and pushing against my leg. I just stood there, listening to the crickets and breathing in the evening air. It was almost June, and Oklahoma summer nights are real soft.